Tragic

Rook and Ronin, Book One

J. A. Huss

Rook and Ronin, Book One

By J. A. Huss
Find me at
New Adult Addiction

Edited by RJ Locksley
Cover design by J. A. Huss

ISBN-13: 978-1-936413-21-8

Books by J.A. Huss

Clutch (I Am Just Junco, Book One)
Fledge (I Am Just Junco, Book Two)
Flight (I Am Just Junco, Book Three)
Range (I Am Just Junco, Book Four)
The Magpie Bridge (A Tier Novella, Book 4.5)
TRAGIC: Rook and Ronin, #1 (May 2013)
Losing Francesca (July 2013)
MANIC: Rook and Ronin, #2 (August 2013)
Return (I Am Just Junco, Book Five) (December 2013)

To anyone who ever wanted to start again.
Just do it, my friend. Just do it.

I have exactly one beta reader, her name is RJ and she's my editor. So, let's all blame her if this book tanks, eh?

Kidding, I'm kidding. Thank you, RJ. You're awesome.

I do everything else myself, including this cover. If you like it, I'll take a bow. If not, oh well. I tried.

I have more to say, but I put that shit in the back now, I tend to go on for a while.

Chapter One

Rook

Life. Sucks.

I step off the curb, dodge a few cars, and head straight for the Starbucks. I can't even remember the last time I had Starbucks, but today, with only ten dollars to my name, I'm getting a ten-freaking-dollar coffee. Quality Cleaning can kiss my ass—I might be poor and I might not have a whole lot going for me right now, but I've never been a thief and I've never been a liar. If they want to try and charge me for stealing a ring I never took, they'll get a fight.

I know it was that stupid Delores who stole that ring. I know it. She blamed it on me and now I'm fired, still living out of a homeless shelter, and on the completely wrong side of town.

I take a deep breath and smell the coffee.

Coffee.

I haven't had a decent coffee in like… well, maybe ever. Even in my other life I wasn't the kind of girl who hung out on the trendy side of town. And this place is definitely trendy, lots of bars—and not the kind that have strippers or that look like they only serve old men at eight in the morning. The kind that serve young people who are out looking to get laid on Friday nights. And men who like sports. The baseball stadium is very close, so there are lots of sports bars.

All the people who are going in and out of this Starbucks look like they work around here, like they belong. I look down at my clothes and wonder if I fit in. My jeans are not designer, shit, they're not even Levis. And my hoodie is from the thrift store near the shelter.

Who gives a crap?

I let a young hipster couple exit and then push my way into the crowded shop. The line is long, but I've got time, so I stand there with more patience than pretty much everyone else in that place, and wait my turn. The barista is patient as I ask questions and I order the biggest latte size they have, ask for real cream and hazelnut syrup, and top it off with whip cream instead of foam.

It takes another ten minutes for them to make my frothy drink and then finally, I take a look around for a place to sit. I have to stand for a few minutes but eventually a man leaves a table and I swoop in, sit with my back to the wall, facing the door, and try to pretend I'm just another girl on a break, getting her usual drink before going back to her trendy job.

That I have a job, period. That I'm not out on the streets, that I'm not a victim, that I'm not scared shitless that Jon will somehow find me.

I take a deep breath and let it out like the counselors at the shelter taught me. This fear of Jon is not rational. I realize this. I mean, I've been gone two months now and no one has even come looking. I gave them a fake name at the shelter, but the maid service needed a real name, and I've worked there for six weeks and no one came looking.

And that sorta bugs me because I pretty much disappeared off the face of the Earth and no one even noticed.

It makes me feel small and inconsequential.

I sip my drink as I look around, the hot liquid soothing me and making my day special. I wonder what Charles is doing these days? He's been gone from the shelter for a few weeks now. Had to go back to jail for a week to serve out some sentence for… something. I never asked. Never wanted to know to be honest. And then he just never came back.

It's that way with pretty much everyone at the shelter. They come and they go. Everything is transient. Just like Starbucks. The people come in, get what they need to get through their day, and then they leave.

A four-seater table opens up next to me and a swarm of tall, thin girls sneak in and claim it, sighing in relief that they found a place to sit and chat, tossing their well-conditioned hair, and clasping their well-manicured hands around tall expensive cardboard cups of coffee.

My hair is a dull dark brown. If I take really good care of it, it's shiny and near-black. But it's barely getting minimal care right now, let alone good.

And I just spent my last ten dollars on a coffee so this hair has no hope. I laugh a little under my breath. As if hair was my biggest problem. *You have no money for* food, *Rook.*

Man, I am so stupid.

The beautiful girls, I learn though eavesdropping, are all models. It figures, right? The select few in the world get everything, while the rest of us poor jerks get to scrub toilets for a living just to make enough to buy food and sleep in a homeless shelter at night.

One girl, a red-head with skin as fair and smooth as ivory, complains loudly about the last photographer who refused to let her even do a test shoot, whatever that means. Another girl passes around a business card, all the others talking about how he's an asshole and they've all been turned away. The red-head who was complaining, thinking she is someone special, realizes to my satisfaction that she's as plain and unwanted as the rest.

The blonde with glossy pink lips grabs the card from the other girl's hand and flicks it in the air. I watch as it sails across the table and plunks me in the head. All the girls start laughing in a fit, grab their coffees, and make a quick escape.

I pick up the card and study it. It's thick and white and says:

Antoine Chaput—Photographer of Artful Beings

That's all. No number, no contact information at all. I flip it over and there's some very messy handwriting in blue ink. An address and the words—*Test shoot, 1 PM, May 17.*

Under the address are the words that make my mouth drop open. *$100 per hour if booked.* The *if booked* is underlined, like whoever wrote it was trying to make a point.

I fish out my phone to check the time. Just short of twelve thirty.

Even though the data plan I purchased months ago for emergencies is almost maxed out, I plug the address into the GPS app on my phone and bite my lip as it pulls up the map. It's only a few blocks over and suddenly my sucky day is getting a little brighter. I shrug on my pack and rush out the door, half running with excitement, half with desperation, towards a job I have no chance of ever getting, especially dressed like this.

But for the first time in a very long time, I feel something besides anger and hopelessness and shame.

I feel a spark and I don't get many of those, so no matter what happens, I'm gonna see where it takes me.

It's windy for mid-May and by the time I make the old warehouse building containing the photographer's studio my hair is a freaking mess. I try to smooth it down a little after the heavy lobby door swishes closed behind me, but it's pretty useless.

I climb the stairs to the fourth floor and arrive at Antoine Chaput's translucent glass door very winded and in complete disarray. There are two names on the door. *Antoine Chaput, Photographer*, of course. But underneath it says *Elise Flynn, Stylist.*

I can hear yelling inside.

And crying.

And then things are breaking and I sink to the floor in fear as Jon's fists come into my mind. But it's like a bad car accident on the freeway—something terrible is happening. I refuse to move my feet, I refuse to plug my ears, and despite the fact that I'm scared shitless by whatever is happening behind that door, I can't turn away from my stolen appointment with Antoine Chaput.

A half-naked young girl bursts through the door, wearing only a pair of pretty panties and matching bra, pulling on her expensive designer jeans as she hops down the hallway, and then before she even buttons them up, she tugs a sweatshirt over her head and spies me on the floor in the corner.

"I'd hide from him too! He's such an asshole! I hate

you, Antoine!" she screams. "And I will never," she picks up some anger here, "*never* let you photograph me again, even if you beg me!" She slips on some cute ballet flats, hopping once again to maintain balance, and is about to leave when she has a thought. I can see her thinking because her eyes roll up a little and her head tilts—like she's a cartoon character with a comment bubble coming out of her mouth. "And I'm keeping the lingerie. Asshole!"

She already said he was an asshole, but I suppose when you're that angry a varied vocabulary isn't the first thing on your mind. The irate girl turns back to me then. "You better be ready. He's in a fit today and I'll never work for him again!"

And then she storms down the stairs, dragging her large bag behind her, still swearing and punctuating her one-sided conversation with the occasional, "Ha!" as she descends.

I stare dumbfounded at the empty stairwell wondering what the hell I'm doing here.

"She's overreacting. Don't let her get to you."

I look over at the man with the deep voice and my mouth drops open a little. He is even more beautiful than the girl who just left. To call him well-built doesn't do his body justice and I can see quite a bit of it because he's only half-dressed. In fact, he's still buttoning up his jeans, tucking in his pockets as he stands there next to me.

He catches me eyeing his fingers and laughs. "Sorry, today was supposed to be a sexy shoot." He shrugs it off like he comes out in the hallway buttoning up his pants all the time.

"Uh"—I clear my throat a little—"yeah."

Oh my God, I am so dumb. Uh, yeah? That's all I can think of to say?

He raises one eyebrow at me and reveals a slow smile that climbs up his face. His eyes are an electric blue and they remind me of my own. I've never seen anyone who had blue eyes like mine—I'm not bragging or anything, it's just a feature that I was born with, something that sets me apart. One of the few things actually.

He notices me studying his eyes and then he bends down to me. I instinctively scoot away from him, pushing myself back into the corner as my heart starts to race. He takes the hint and stands back up. "Sorry, didn't mean to invade your space or anything."

Another voice snaps my attention back to what I'm doing. "OK, let's go, girl. Get in here, you heard Clare, he's in a fit. So let's just humor him and maybe we can all go home early, what do you say?"

I nod, still cowering on the floor.

"Oh, come now." A petite woman with short-cropped blonde hair pushes the half-naked guy out of the way and continues talking. "He's already cooling off. Clare pushes his buttons, everyone knows she's difficult. Do you have your invitation?"

She's looking at the card in my hand so I stand and thrust it at her. Half-naked guy is still watching me and just as I'm about to brush past his bare chest, he stops me with a hand on my arm. I pull it away quickly. "Don't."

"Sweetheart, you won't get far here if we can't touch you."

I scowl at him and swallow hard.

"It's a test shoot, Ronin, don't get her worked up." And then the woman takes my hand and leads me inside.

Ronin mumbles out a response as he follows and then the door closes behind me and I expect all manner of terrible things to start happening, but all the woman does is push me over to what looks like a shampoo station. She takes my bag, tucks it into a corner, and then motions me into a changing area and tells me to take off my hoodie.

I look around for Ronin, but he's disappeared. "But I don't have anything on underneath."

"Nothing?"

I shake my head.

"Well, that's not very smart." She rummages through a drawer and throws a tank top at me. "Put that on."

I do and before I can even turn the corner of the little screened-in changing area, she's pushing me back into the chair. "I don't know who your stylist is—what did you say your name was?"

"Rook Walsh," I say weakly.

"Oh, yes. I remember now," she says as she picks up the ends of my very long hair, "*Rook*. You need to tell that stylist of yours that these ends need a touch-up. Antoine prefers *au naturel*, but it must be healthy—so trim these ends if he invites you back. Today is just a test shoot, but we've got good light coming in the afternoon and you know how Antoine loves *au naturel* light." She winks at me and I laugh.

"I'm Elise, by the way. Antoine's lover."

She says it so casually, this word. *Lover*. It implies so much more than girlfriend. *Lover*. It drips with sex. I smile at her. "Nice to meet you—"

But she's dousing me with water and my words get lost in the feeling of having my hair washed by a professional again. In the shelter I'm lucky if I get a shower twice a week. You have to work in the kitchen for three days to get one shower. But I had one last night, so I'm not too dirty.

Elise's fingertips start massaging my head and then she squirts some tropical-smelling shampoo on it. She lathers it up, starting at the bottom and then working the thick froth into my scalp. It feels so good I almost moan with pleasure.

Then the rinse again. The water trickles down my scalp, sometimes a stray stream will slide down the edge of my cheek and it sends a shiver up my whole body. I feel myself relax just as Elise wrings out the excess water and then very carefully works the conditioner in.

"Long day, Rook?" she asks me.

"Yeah," I reply, sedated and warm. "I got fired today."

"Oh, I'm sorry. It's hard to make it as a model, I know. When I was just starting out I had to work all sorts of odd jobs. Waitressing, bartender, I was even a tow truck dispatcher at night. Whatever it took to keep my nail appointments and have a nice wardrobe. I suppose it's that way for you now, huh?"

I open my eyes. "Sorta."

"What kind of job was it?"

"Cleaning houses."

"Oh, yeah, I've done that too, those were the worst. I got accused of stealing once, and I never even took anything."

I try to sit up but she pushes me back down. "Me too! I didn't take that ring, Delores did, and they fired me."

She clicks her tongue at me and shakes her head. "Well, you're pretty enough and skinny enough and your legs and hair are long. Antoine likes all these features you have—so if you just do exactly what he tells you, maybe you'll find a better job today. Right?"

"I'd like that," I whisper.

Elise smiles. "You're not like the others, Rook. You're calm and quiet, and a bit tragic, if you don't mind me saying."

"I don't mind it." *Because it's true*, I don't add.

"Antoine is hard to work for, I won't lie. But you might do, so just keep your mouth shut and do everything he asks."

I nod as the water sprays down my face again and keep my mouth shut for the rest of the time. I catch that Ronin guy walking around a little in the part of the studio I can see. He looks over at me each time, almost stopping to take a second look as Elise pulls and tugs my hair through her various brushes.

He's watching me.

Chapter Two

Ronin

I leave Elise with the new girl and join Antoine in his office. As older sisters go I could do a lot worse than Elise, and since she raised me since I was ten, I am eternally grateful and only want her to be happy. But honestly, Antoine drives me up a wall. She's been dating him forever, so he practically raised me as well, but a father figure he is *not.*

Describing him as an artist should really do the trick—he's got all the stereotypical attributes like selfish, asshole, romantic, asshole, creative, asshole, temperamental, asshole. I could go on and on, but what's the point. He's an asshole.

And since he refused to speak to me and Elise in anything but French for the first five years we all lived together, we're both now fluent.

So I guess I can thank him for that.

But French is a pretty stupid language to know when you live in Denver. Maybe if I move to Quebec or Paris it might come in handy. And actually, we did go to Paris with him last year to do a show, but he hates it there just as much we did, so I doubt we'll be going back.

He speaks more English now, but that's only because he has to talk to more people than just Elise and me. Back when he was just starting out it was just us, so he could get by without speaking English if he wanted. But now, Antoine Chaput is big time and he's got a lot of people keeping this place going.

And none of them speak French.

"She'll get over it, Antoine," I tell him as I take a seat across from his desk. "Just let her walk out."

Antoine is running his hands through his hair, messing it all up and making himself look ridiculous, but he is about to flip out over this Clare shit, I can tell, so I run interference. "She's on the rag today, she told me. And you know how bitchy she is on the rag."

She doesn't have her period today, she's just a raging bitch and not in her right mind every day, but this puts the blame on her instead of him, and that's what he wants—so fuck it. I give him what he wants to keep the peace.

"She's done. I don't want to see her again! No more!"

I shrug. He says this at least once a month. Clare walks out pissed off all the time when we let her work, it's nothing new or extraordinary. They do this dance so often, it's like a couple of dorky kids doing the box-step at senior prom.

I reach over and grab an apple off the perpetual fruit basket Antoine has on his desk and take a seat in the deep leather couch that gives me a full view of the studio so I can watch for the new girl. Antoine is still mumbling about Clare.

"English, Antoine," I say as I chew.

"Ne pas parler la bouche pleine!"

"Clare's only purpose in life right now is to drive you crazy, let her go." I swallow so he'll stop concentrating on the food in my talking mouth and listen to my words instead. "Fuck her. There's a new girl out there, did you see her?"

He perks up at this, but then he sighs and collapses into his desk chair. "No. She's probably no good. I have no one for this campaign. No one."

"She'll work, Antoine. She's tall, thin, black hair, blue eyes—like mine," I add, because my eyes look like someone got carried away with the special effects in a sci-fi movie. My peepers have made me quite a bit of cash over the past few years and the fact that this girl has eyes like mine is pretty interesting. "If ever there was a girl who is crying out that she's TRAGIC, it's this one. Just wait until you see her."

I take another bite of apple and he sighs, trying to peek out the door and see something, but not be noticed for noticing. I can hear them talking, just faintly, but I'm intrigued. "Want me to go spy?" I ask, smiling.

"*Oui*," he grins back.

That grin says we have to stick together or they will overpower us. They being woman, us being men. He's forever on this guy thing with me, like we are in some secret fraternal society—sometimes these secret plans even come with a wink. I let him have his fun and get up to go spy. I want to see her again anyway. Before she comes out and has to pretend to be someone else.

"I want a full report, and don't let Ellie see you, or she'll complain to me later."

"*Oui*," I reply.

Chapter Three

Ronin

I sit on a stool near the entrance to Elise's studio and eat my apple, chewing casually as I watch Ed and Alex mess with some sets. They have a whole team of people to handle the lights and move shit around, but this is all for the TRAGIC campaign, not this girl's test shoot.

If you're lucky enough to get an invitation from Antoine to come sit for him, you get one shot to make him fall in love. If he does, you might get another invitation, but only if he has an immediate need for you. If he doesn't love you at first sight, i.e. if he needs Elise to make you pretty or alluring, or sexy, or tragic—whatever—he won't ever ask you back. Elise is here to bring out the mood he wants, like a make-up artist in the movies. She's not here to make you into the thing Antoine is looking for. Either you are that thing, or you're not.

And I know this girl is tragic. He's gonna love her because I've watched Antoine choose hundreds of girls over the past twelve years and I love her.

Her look, I clarify to myself. I love *her look*.

I toss my apple core into a nearby wastebasket and listen in as the girls talk on the other side of the partitioned wall. Elise will have to fill me in later because I can't really make out what they're saying.

Test shoots last for about an hour or so, sometimes less. Sometimes more, but if Antoine goes over an hour with you on a test shoot, he's definitely in love with you.

When Elise went for her test shoot he took pictures of her for five hours. Then he made us move in with him so she'd never leave. He fell hard for her even though she's nothing like any of the models that come through the studio. She's small, tiny really, she has the most severe pixie haircut to match her fairy frame, and she's quiet and graceful. She's like a little dancer, not a bitchy model like Clare.

And that's how I know Antoine is a good guy, even if he does act like an asshole most of the time.

He loves my sister. And my sister is good people.

I get up and walk casually towards the front door, which is located just a few steps away from Elise's station, and peek in as I walk by. Elise starts shaking her head at me as I watch the girl hide under her long hair. Elise has it all combed over her head in different ways, trying to partition it off for blow-drying. They don't talk now, the dryer is too loud, but I'm pretty sure the girl is watching me from under her hair. I can see the brightness of her eyes.

I continue walking and go through the door, then jog down the stairs and go out to the street. It's just a way to pass time and it will give me another excuse to walk past again in a few minutes when I go back up.

Downstairs it's busy because there's a baseball game today. We rent out our parking lot out on game days since we're practically across the street from the stadium. Our lot is already full, the attendants standing guard to prevent anyone else from coming in. The streets are packed with people and there are lots of bars and restaurants to make the place look safe and trendy. And for the most part, it is. But at night, you do not want to be a girl alone in this neighborhood.

I wave to a couple of guys I recognize from elementary school standing on a corner handing out flyers. Probably for a party this weekend.

Our building is an old factory that Antoine bought back when the property values in Five Points were shit. It's six stories tall, but we gutted the top three floors to create the massive windows that allow for natural light to pour into the studio. It's all about the light with Antoine. One half of the sixth floor contains our apartments. I have one and Elise and Antoine have one. There's a large open terrace off the studio where we do most of our outside shots. Most of the other floors are either empty or used for artistic shoots.

The neighborhood has grown up with the new stadium. It used to be pretty bad, but after living here in Antoine's studio for the past twelve years, this building and neighborhood, crime statistics and all, is the only place I'd ever call home. I people-watch for a few more minutes, then head back up and enter the studio just as Elise is tugging the girl across the room. I want to talk to her so bad, but I catch Antoine in the doorway to his office and Elise jerks her head at me as she tells the girl to wait near the window.

I watch her walk and look over at Antoine again. He's smiling, but he's talking in French about Clare. She called him and gave him an earful and I know from the tone of his voice that Clare is wearing him down, weaseling her way back into another job. I sigh and follow Elise to try and calm Antoine's nerves.

The new girl will have to wait a little longer because no matter how many times I tell myself I don't give one fucking shit about Clare, I can't help myself. I still do.

Chapter Four

Elise walks towards Antoine, but turns back when I start to follow. "Go over to the window, he wants to shoot by the window today. And just do what you're told, OK?"

I nod and she walks away with a brisk pace as I make my way to the window, looking up and gawking at how magnificent this place is.

Studio is not really the right word for it, it's several stories tall, and now that I think about it, it's the top floor of the building, even though we're only on the fourth floor of what appears to be a six-story building on the outside. There's a long modern staircase made up of concrete stairs and metal railings that leads up the far side of the room near Antoine's office, and the second story is loft-like with a set of double doors in the middle of the open hallway.

When I turn to the windows, I can totally see why Antoine would want to shoot pictures over here. They are massive. Two stories tall, each ten feet wide and the golden sunshine pouring through them lights the whole place up like heaven. Like angels with trumpets are about to fly in and celebrate the beauty that is this room.

The floors are a polished warm oak, and the whole place is filled with different set-ups. Like sets or something for photographers. Ladders and those umbrella things that you see in photo shoots to reflect light this way and that.

Antoine, Ronin, and Elise are arguing in the back room, but I can't understand them because they are all speaking French. Suddenly the door slams and I jump a little at the noise, but then enjoy the silence as they finish their argument in private. I'm sure Antoine took one look at me and refused to even bother getting out his camera.

I peer through the window and enjoy the view. It's spectacular and looks out onto a busy street. There are a few tall buildings nearby, but it's mostly small businesses contained within old historic buildings—various stores, restaurants, and bars. I watch the people below, going about their lives. I watch the women in particular. How many of them have lived with abuse? I try not to think about it really. It's over now. It's behind me and I'm sorta moving on. There have been a few incidents at the shelter with some of the druggie men, but I have a knife. I cut one guy across the arm when he touched me in my sleep. Since then they've left me alone.

I hate that place though. And all these women over on this side of town seem happy. I'm sure there are plenty of them who suffer abuse and are good at hiding it like I was, but from this vantage point, it seems unlikely that they are anywhere near the type of situation I was in back in Chicago.

Jon and I met in high school. Well, I was in high

school, and that's only on a technicality because I never actually *went* to school. He was five years older. I realize now that lots of abusers look for young girls because they are easier to control and scare into silence, but at the time I just thought it was cool that an older guy liked me. He thought I was sexy, he told me things no boy ever told me. He treated me like a woman even though I was a girl.

I liked it at first. That he was tall and strong. He had his own place, a car, a job, a brand new college degree. It seemed like a perfect opportunity for me. A way to escape my stressful life and let someone else think about all these things people require for survival for once. No teenager should have to worry about living day to day the way I did.

So I let him take care of me. And maybe for a little while I could fool myself into thinking his strange obsession with controlling everything about me was normal, or a way to express his love.

But then his fists got involved, and by that time I was so dependent on him there wasn't a chance in hell I could make it on my own any more. He never lifted a hand to me at first, but slowly, over the course of several months, he alienated me from the few friends I had, asked me to quit my job, and moved us out to the country where he had access to a small family home that was sitting unoccupied.

And that's when it all changed. He spied on me, he monitored things like gas and groceries. Weird shit. And I was just too stupid to figure it out. Or just too young maybe.

Life in Chicago was the only life I knew before coming to Denver. It started out better than it ended up, that's for sure. I used to have a family. A mom at least. But she's been gone for a while now. I have nothing left of her, not even a picture. So the image of her burned into my memory is all that I have.

I'm pretty sure that memory is a bit skewed. For example, I picture her in a dress with an apron, but I'm almost positive that I'm thinking of one of the moms on RetroTube at night, and not my mother.

My mother didn't bake pies, she smoked crack.

But that's what happens when all you have left is a memory. Things change over time, other memories and images invade and reshape it.

You forget things.

And mostly you tend to forget bad things and I find that to be dangerous. Because if you forget the bad things, chances are those bad things will come back to get you again.

I try really hard to keep my memories of living with Jon fresh so I don't forget.

And I don't even care if this is healthy or whatever. The counselors at the shelter hinted that it's best to let the past go, but I don't agree and it's my life, my death. So I'm the one who gets to make the final decision.

I feel satisfied at that because I love making my own decisions.

Like today, for instance. I walked out of that job after they accused me of stealing. They did fire me first, and I could've stayed and groveled, but I didn't. I walked away.

Now I'm homeless, jobless, and broke. But at least I'm not scared and at least I'm not broken and at least I'm not letting people who know nothing about me dictate who and what I am. Even though I spend my nights with drug addicts and criminals, and probably rapists and maybe even murderers—I am less afraid in that shelter than I was at home with my ex-boyfriend.

The noise of a camera shutter snaps me back to

reality. "No, don't move, Rook. You're perfect right there."

I take my attention back to the window and the memories, ignoring Antoine. If that's what he wants, then fuck it. What do I care? This whole thing is probably a set-up anyway, to get me to do porn movies or something.

The shutter continues to snap, but Antoine becomes more and more chatty. Directing me to move my arm, or tilt my head, or close my eyes, or frown.

I do it all just like he asks. Just like Elise told me to.

And I never once smile.

And he never once asks me to.

"What are you thinking about, Rook?" Antoine says later, when he's fussing with his camera and everyone else except that Ronin guy has left.

I look over at Antoine. He's tall and thick. Not fat by any means, just thick. His hair is dark and his eyes are blue, like mine, like that Ronin guy. He's wearing dark jeans and a black t-shirt, and for an older guy, late thirties maybe, he's handsome. Not hot or cute, but definitely handsome in a chiseled jaw and scratchy face kind of way.

I can see why Elise is his lover.

"None of your business," I answer him after my pause.

His reaction is lost on me because I turn back to the window.

"Do you enjoy modeling?"

I shrug. "It's a job."

"Do you have a book?"

I have no idea what that means so I just say, "No."

This time his reaction is not lost on me because he bellows out a laugh. "No? If you're a model you have a book. Show it to me." He pulls out a card and offers it.

"Here is my e-mail, send me your photos."

I take the card and meet his eyes this time. "I am not a model and I have no book, whatever that is. I just need a job. The invitation card said $100 an hour. I just need the money."

"Test shoots pay in pictures, child. You don't get paid for today, but I'll give you a CD with your images, just give me your address and I'll send it when it's ready."

I'm the one who bellows out a laugh this time. "Pictures? I don't need any fucking pictures! I need money!" I walk back over to the style station and Elise is watching me with a nervous expression. "Where's my bag? I'm leaving. What a waste of time. Pictures!"

My hoodie is still in the little changing area and I whip the tank top off and pull the thrift store bargain over my head. When I come out from behind the partition I thrust the shirt at Elise. "Here."

She accepts it and I grab my bag and walk out the door.

Pictures!

What a load of shit! I just wasted my whole day, I'm on the wrong side of town, I'll never get back to the shelter in time to get a bed, and I have no money to even take the bus because I needed a ten-dollar coffee from freaking Starbucks!

I descend the stairs as fast as I can and when I get to the bottom I just stand in front of the heavy oak door, unsure of what to do next.

I collapse on the bottom step and start to cry.

Chapter Five

Ronin

Her name is Rook. She's wrecked, those were Elise's words. She and Antoine are fighting over the TRAGIC campaign. Elise says no way, Antoine says she's the only one that can do it. With one look out his door, he picked her. He fell in photographer love with her.

I smile to myself thinking of his words, because I knew it.

We need her.

But Elise has power in this house. Elise, no matter what Antoine says, wears the pants in their relationship because if Elise is unhappy Antoine cannot live with himself. He falls to pieces when they fight.

So we work on her for almost half an hour inside the office. We wear her down, we make promises. We will watch Rook, we promise. We won't push her, we'll be careful. We promise all these things if Elise will let us keep this girl.

We want her that bad.

Of course, for very different reasons. Antoine wants to shoot her, I want to keep her. Antoine wants to take pictures of her gorgeous body and her fragile face, but I want to peel away her layers and see what's underneath. Antoine wants to make her famous and I want to hide her away in my room, under the covers of my bed, under me.

By the time we get Elise to agree to our plan, I'm half afraid the girl might've left, but as soon as we open the door she's there, next to the window where Elise left her. She's looking outside, so deep in thought she hears nothing. Not the dozens of workers who mill about in her immediate vicinity and certainly not us as we extract ourselves, full of longing (Antoine), pity (Elise) and desire (me).

We walk up behind her and still her gaze remains fixed on the people down below. You can just see she's not with us, that her thoughts are spinning and her life is chaos. It's written all over her face and Antoine sighs as he sees it too. I can read these girls almost as well as he can by now—that's my job. To get them worked up—to make these girls feel things—to bring those feelings out. Paint those feelings on their faces so when Antoine lifts his camera he's not capturing the body, but the mind.

That's why he's famous. It's not the body or face, it's the emotion. The emotion *I* make them feel.

I want to touch her right now but I hold back with Elise as Antoine starts shooting. The noise of the shutter snaps her out of her daze and I expect her to say something.

Anything—like *Am I doing it right? Is this what you want?*

But she says nothing. Antoine whispers to her, giving her small directions. She tilts her head when he asks, letting the light from the window fall across her face. It's late afternoon now, so the light is low and hazy. It bounces off her raven hair and her head turns in just the right way to catch some dying rays of sun, making her eyes sparkle. And that's how she's burned into my mind. The blackness of her hair, contrasting with the gray light behind her, and her bright blue eyes.

She catches me staring and I hold my breath. But neither of us turns away. We stare, unabashed, until Antoine's direction pulls her back into the shoot and she's lost again—guarded and unhappy, frowning and resigned. She's a blackbird sitting in a tree staring out at the world, daring the wind to come and knock her off the swaying bough.

She is wrecked, Elise is right. But she's not down yet. The look on her face is defiant.

When I look over at the clock it's well past five. Antoine has been shooting her for almost two hours. Elise left a while back but whether she's still here in the studio or up in her apartment, I have no idea. I lost track of her because my eyes are only on the girl.

Antoine does pretty well until the end. It's clear he's finished shooting and the girl is starting to look uncomfortable when he asks her what she was thinking about during the shoot.

I cringe. *No, you don't ask them! You make them want to tell you, you idiot!* I want to pull him aside and stop the crash and burn that's coming, but it's too late. She snaps at him and he pulls back when he realizes his mistake.

He turns the conversation to business and this is where it really gets interesting. She tells him she's not a model and has no portfolio. I'm just about to laugh when she starts yelling about pictures as payment.

I look back towards Elise's station and realize she forgot to explain the terms to her.

We are so off our game today. One tragic girl has disrupted all the carefully laid plans and protocols we've had in place for years.

The tragic girl storms off yelling. Antoine walks over to me and we wait together as she rants to Elise.

"You better fix this, Antoine," I say calmly, but inside I'm screaming too. "Pay the fucking girl, she needs the money."

He snorts like a fucking Frenchman. "I do not pay for test shoots."

"This," I say, turning to face him, "was no test shoot and you know it. You've got hundreds of shots in that camera. Pay her and make sure she comes back or I won't do the contract. I want her. I've put up with hundreds of stupid girls over the years for you and I've never asked you for a favor like this. I want this one, or I won't do it."

He fishes through his pocket and pulls out the cash that Clare never earned.

The studio door slams and we are all reminded that two models have walked out on us today.

"Elise!" Antoine calls, thrusting the bills out at her. "Catch her, pay her, and invite her back on Monday."

Elise grabs the money and flies out the door.

"We're in trouble, Ronin. She is trouble." He turns a little to look me in the eye, something he rarely does unless he's serious and wants me to consider his advice. "You should stay away from her, keep it professional. Or it might get messy."

I shrug. "I'll do what I want. And staying away from her isn't even in the top million things I want to do with that girl."

"Elise will hurt you if you ruin this one, Ronin. She won't tolerate another Mardee."

Fuck you, is what I think. But I don't say it, I just sigh and we wait in silence for Elise to come back.

Chapter Six

My crying is not pretty, in fact, it borders on blubbering. It's a sobbing ugly cry, except I'm trying to be discreet so it comes out in weird half-silent gasps, in between hiccups and long draws of air.

When I hear footsteps I pull myself together, wipe the tears, and scoot over so whoever it is can get by. Instead they sit down next to me.

I look over at Elise and she holds out some money. "Here. He really doesn't pay for test shoots, Rook, but he likes your look and would like to extend another invitation." I take the bills and see that on top there is another little white card. I know I shouldn't, but I count the money as I sit there. Four hundred dollars in twenties. One hundred dollars for every hour I spent here today.

I look at her and start to cry again.

I know I should get up and just bolt out the door with my money, just make a quick getaway and leave this day behind, but Elise grabs my arm before I can stand up and I just don't have it in me to fight. I collapse back against the stairs and wipe my face frantically.

"Do you need help?" Elise asks after giving me a few moments to stop the tears.

I do. I mean, I really do. But I'm ashamed to have to ask for it. "No," comes out automatically.

She rubs my arm and lets out a small laugh. "OK. Well, would you believe that I am actually looking for someone to help *me* in the studio salon?"

I raise my tired and burning eyes up to her in surprise.

"Yes," she nods at me. "I am desperate, Rook. And I realize this is forward of me, but you did say you got fired today, so I was wondering if you'd like the job?"

"A job?"

"Shampoo girl. It's not much and it pays very little, but it does come with a small apartment out on the roof terrace."

"An apartment?"

"I know what you're thinking. Is the apartment nice? But I'm afraid, no, it's not. It's tiny really, and filled with old furniture. You'll probably hate it and I'm embarrassed to even offer it, but I figured you might take pity on me and accept the position and the apartment."

I just stare at her.

"What do you say?"

I cry.

She wraps her arm around me and laughs. "Just say yes, Rook. And we'll go back upstairs and you can go settle in that terribly ugly and small living space and try to forget this whole day." She stands and takes me with her and we begin to climb the stairs. "Except for the part where you got your hands on that invitation card and met us, of course. Because maybe tomorrow you'll see this was a stroke of luck for you."

She knew all along that wasn't my invitation, yet she pretended to remember me when I gave her my name. "Why are you doing this? I mean, I'm grateful and I want the job and the apartment, I really do. But you don't even know me."

"I've been you, Rook. I don't know the details, but we've all needed a twist of fate at one time or another and Antoine was mine. More than twelve years ago now. So today, I'll pay it back and be yours."

"Thank you."

"And one day, you'll be in my position and you'll stumble upon a lost girl, and you can help change her fate. And when you do, and she asks you why, you'll tell her about me."

We walk up the rest of the stairs in silence after that and when she takes me through the studio door we come face to face with Antoine and that Ronin guy again. Elise says something in French, and then they are all talking in French. But Elise does not wait for them, because she walks me around the other side of the salon wall and takes me through the massive glass doors that lead out onto the terrace.

It's one of the most beautiful places I've ever seen. Somehow, even though this is a rooftop terrace, there are two small groves of blooming cherry trees on either side. There's even grass on the ground under the trees. "How is there grass up here?" I ask as we walk past the trees and head towards a small brick building on the far side of the terrace.

"My Antoine is clever," she snickers. "It used to be a lap pool on one side," she points to the east where the sky is already getting dark, "and a family pool on the other." She points west now, towards the mountains and the setting sun. "Some developers bought this building from the city and made it into apartments back in the Seventies, but when we bought it more than a decade ago, the pools were a disaster, so instead of filling them in with concrete, we filled them in with dirt and planted those cherry trees and grass. We add something to the landscaping every year, usually another fruit tree."

It's like Mary Lennox's Secret Garden. Except it's on a rooftop in a trendy Denver neighborhood instead of the English countryside. I feel a little sad for a moment, because of all the people living in this city, only a handful of them will ever get a chance to walk through an orchard four stories up on the top of an old building.

Elise stops at the small apartment and punches in a number on the keypad. "All our doors have keyed locks. I'll bring you a code to use for the outside building after hours, but the garden studio apartment is all ones. Just five ones."

"OK." It sounds very fancy, but I can deal with five ones.

"And I might've lied a bit about the apartment."

"Oh," I say, the disappointment coming out.

"It's actually very cute. Not big, I didn't lie about that, but—" She opens the door and waves me inside.

It's the most darling place I've ever seen. The walls are painted a sunny yellow, the furniture is older, that wasn't a lie, but it's got a pretty flower pattern on it and it looks very comfortable. There's a couch, an overstuffed chair in the same pattern, a coffee table made out of oak, and two end tables. The kitchen is small, just one long counter against the far wall. There's a fridge and a small apartment-sized stove. When I look down the hallway I can see a bed dressed up in the same pattern as the living room furniture.

"It's not really a studio because it has a bedroom, but

there's no door. So it's like a loft, I guess. The bathroom has a giant claw-foot tub."

I moan with happiness. "This cannot come with the shampoo girl's job."

Elise laughs. "No, I lied about that too. But if you play your cards right, Antoine and Ronin will choose you for the TRAGIC campaign and you'll be wanting to move out and get a penthouse apartment in New York like the last girl who lived here before you know it."

"The last girl?"

Elise nods. "She's the one who decorated the place, just secondhand stuff from consignment shops on the west side of town. But it's cute, right?"

It is, so I nod. There are many windows so even in the approaching darkness I can see how much light comes in.

"I don't even know what to say, Elise. I mean—" I'm truly at a loss for words. "I'm not sure how this happened. I didn't steal that invitation, I was just minding my own business over at Starbucks and these girls flipped the card away, and it hit me in the head, and—"

"It doesn't matter, Rook. That girl was never going to get asked back after her test shoot. She got an invitation as a favor to her agency. Antoine does not mess around with the models he uses. I told you he'd like your look and I was right. Now, my brother Ronin—"

Oh, I say to myself, blocking out her words but still smiling politely as she talks. Ronin is her *brother*. That's interesting.

"—so he's the one you'll want to worry about after Antoine makes his decision."

"Worry about?" I missed that. I hope she repeats it.

"Never mind him for now. Just stay out of his way, do what you're told, and don't act like the girl you watched storm out of here earlier."

"Clare?"

Elise rolls her eyes. "Yes, Clare. She's talented and has a long list of clients who want her for glamour and fashion contracts, but she's crossing lines with all of us, making Antoine very angry."

"And Ronin?"

"No, Ronin rarely gets angry with the girls. Now, I hate to do this to you, but Antoine and I are going up to the mountains for the weekend, so I have to rush out. But make yourself at home and I'll leave the building code with Ronin. I'm sure he'll be partying all weekend but Cookie's Diner down the street has a tab for our girls so you can go eat there. Just tell the hostess you belong to Ronin and it will be taken care of."

Oh, that makes my face blush! I wonder if I could even force those words to come out of my mouth? *I belong to Ronin.* It's sexy and sexist at the same time. Do I like that? I'm not sure. I'm definitely not Ronin's, that I know. I might like to look at his half-naked body, but I'm nowhere close to wanting him near me. He's one of those over-confident players, I can just tell.

And I'm not a player or even slightly confident, so I'd probably make my life a lot easier if I take Elise's advice and stay out of his way.

Before I can pull myself back to reality to keep the conversation going, Elise is making for the door and shouting out, "See you Monday."

And then I stand there. Alone.

Feeling very much like Cinder-freaking-ella.

Chapter Seven

Elise is brimming with delight as she finds Antoine and I munching on apples in his office. "You want to explain what just happened?" I ask her.

She closes the door, still smiling. "I saved her, that's all."

"Saved her how, exactly?" Antoine questions.

"She's a mess, I think she's homeless or at the very least, not willing to go home. I gave her the garden apartment and a job washing hair in the salon."

"Washing hair!" Antoine and I bellow it together.

Elise puts her hands up like she's warding off our complaints. "She was too proud to admit she needed help, so I made it easier for her to accept it, that's all."

"So, she's not the new shampoo girl?"

"No, Ronin, she is. She has to be, or she might bolt and get a hotel room with her money or something."

"Elise, we want her for TRAGIC, she can't be shampooing hair. The other girls will swoop in like lions, she'll walk out!"

"Well, then I suggest you get those girls under control, Ronin. You let them get away with far too much. If they're mean to her and she walks out, that's your fault. Now." My tiny little sister rubs her hands together and seats herself in Antoine's lap and cups his face. "I'm ready for the mountains. Take me up there and rock my world."

"Oh, sick! You two!" Oh God, they're kissing now! "I'm leaving, does this girl need a babysitter, or what? I don't have to stick around, do I?"

I roll my eyes as Antoine and Elise finish their kiss.

"No, but she needs an exterior building code so she can come and go as she pleases," Elise says, breathless from her kiss. "Can you take her a code? I have to pack." And then she skips out of the office and heads for her and Antoine's apartment upstairs.

I look over at Antoine. His one brow is lifted all the way up to his forehead.

"What?"

"This girl, Ronin. You know what."

"Hey, you liked her too, it's not just me. She's perfect, right? She's the same type of girl you described to me last week, only that was your fantasy girl for TRAGIC. She's like a little modeling-god gift. Don't jinx it."

He's not convinced. "Elise wants to save her and you will ruin her. This will not turn out well."

"What do you mean? I have no intention of *ruining* her!"

"You know exactly what I mean. TRAGIC is named tragic for a reason. You're going to ruin this girl."

"You have no idea what you're talking about. I take care of *all* of these girls."

"You didn't take care of Mardee."

My mouth drops open, that's how stunned I am that he went there. "Antoine, dude, seriously, you're pissing me off now. What happened to her had nothing to do with me."

"No?" he asks evenly. "You brought her in here and she was swept up in the life. This Rook girl is Mardee all over again. I can see it. She's sweet and innocent now, but just wait until the money starts rolling in and the men start making offers. The agencies will be circling like vultures to get to her. It takes a strong person to navigate the maze of predators in this world, you know that."

"I told you, I'll manage her. Shit."

"You better, Ronin. Because Elise is invested in this one and that means I'm invested in her now, too. I won't stand by like last time."

"Get the hell out of here. You need a vacation. I take care of all these girls. Ask any one of them." He makes to protest and I add in, "Besides Clare! Clare doesn't count, so do not even start with me on her."

He gets up from his chair and points to his fruit basket. "Put that in the kitchen, will you? I don't want it to go to waste while we're out of town."

"Sure," I say, relieved that he's dropping the whole Mardee thing. I pick up the basket and head out, trying to shake off the feeling of shame that Mardee's name brings out in me.

She *was* out of control but I wasn't in charge of her personal life. Hell, I was only nineteen myself back then. I had just started managing the girls. It was hardly my fault that Mardee fell in with the neighborhood scum.

Besides, I've made a lot of changes since then.

I will not have a repeat of Mardee.

The kitchen is clean and quiet now that Friday afternoon has passed into Friday evening. I stick the basket of fruit in the fridge with the others so it will keep over the weekend. Antoine is a fanatic about his fruit baskets. My gaze wanders to the large window over the sink and I spy Rook's garden apartment. She has the curtains open wide and she's standing in front of it, looking out on the cherry trees.

I have to agree with Antoine. This girl is a Mardee waiting to happen and I should really make myself available tonight so she doesn't wander off and get in trouble in the rowdy neighborhood.

But why? She has no building code, so she can't leave. I smile as the idea comes to me. I'll just conveniently forget to take her the code and then I can enjoy my Friday night without having to wonder if her skinny ass needs saving. Yes, this might be easier than I thought.

I leave the kitchen, take the stairs three at time, and walk the hallway down to my apartment.

Rook can't get into trouble if she never gets the chance.

Sounds like a perfect plan to me.

What could go wrong?

Elise never appears with my building code and I'm starving. My stomach is churning with the emptiness, that's how hungry I am. The only thing I ate today was, well, a ten-dollar latte at Starbucks doesn't count as food, really. So I have not eaten anything today.

I peek out the window at the studio building. From the front room I can see the two-story windows on the fourth and fifth floors, and then on the sixth floor, there are smaller windows. There was a light on in one a few hours ago, but now everything is dark. I'm pretty sure there's a kitchen inside, but my code for the garden apartment won't open the doors that go into the studio.

So I'm like a prisoner out here in the secret garden.

I'm a secret prisoner.

It makes me uncomfortable. I mean, I really don't know these people at all. I met them today and the one I talked to has left for the weekend and the one who was supposed to take care of things is nowhere to be found. I wander the massive garden terrace. Pace, actually. I pace the terrace. And what's worse is that I can hear all sorts of people down below. This building is smack in the middle of a very active area of Denver filled with bars and all sorts of nightlife.

And I'm a secret prisoner in a secret garden.

I walk along the edge of the terrace and peer over to see what's happening down there. Lots of people. Lots of loud people which in my experience means lots of drunk people. Down the street is a huge neon sign that flashes an image of a Fifties waitress and the letters, *Cookie's Diner!* If I get down I can go to Cookie's and tell them I belong to Ronin and get free food.

Screw that, I have money. I don't need to belong to Ronin to feed myself.

I huff out some air and start to get annoyed. My stomach hurts, dammit! I look up at the window where the lights were one more time and spy a fire escape. Am I that desperate that I'm thinking about using the fire escape?

My feet are already across the terrace and I'm hopping over the short iron railing that allows access to the stairs. I've never been on a fire escape. I grew up in foster homes and maybe Chicago isn't the best place to be a foster kid, but they always placed me in actual houses, I'll give them that.

But I've seen them on TV. You just hop over, climb down, and then hang onto that ladder thing at the bottom where it delivers you safely to the ground. Easy. My feet bang down the metal stairs and when I get to the last level there's a lever that looks like it wants to be pulled. I release it and the ladder drops down to the ground.

I am minutes away from food!

But voices down the alley stop me. There's a group of guys just turning the corner. If I hustle I can get down on the ground and be back out on the busy street before they get close. I climb down and they start calling out to me.

Shit, Rook! This is not a good situation to be in. I drop to the ground and make my way out to the street. The people are still loud and there's even more of them than there were before, but at least I'm not alone in a dark alley.

Cookie's is on the other side of the street, but that's the busy side where all the bars are, so I keep to my side and walk down the block, shoving my hand in my pocket to grab my money.

Shit again! I look back up at the Chaput Building wistfully. My money is still upstairs. I am so stupid. I turn around to go back up the fire escape to get my money and see the rowdy guys from the alley turn the corner.

I spin around and make my way to Cookie's. I guess for tonight I'll belong to Ronin. I weave my way through the crowds, looking back nervously as the guys follow me, and then cross the street when I get to the corner.

A hand grabs me from behind and I jerk away and turn. "Get your hands off me!"

The guy is tall and has a surprised look on his face. "Sorry, geez. We just wanted to see if you're OK. You look pretty shook up."

He's not one of the guys from the alley because they are still across the street. I turn away again, not caring if I was rude because I'm just totally out of my element right now and I just want to get something to eat. A crowd exits the diner and I let them jostle me away from the offended guy and push me inside. When the door closes behind me I let out a huge breath of relief.

Cookie's Diner right now is a haven for me. Some of the sound from outside is muffled and I give myself a moment to relax before the door opens and lets the noise back in.

"Can I help ya, honey?" the middle-aged waitress asks me as I stand there breathing hard.

"Um." Shit. I suck it up and force the words out. "I belong to Ronin and I just want some food to go, if that's OK."

The waitress smiles and winks at someone in the doorway behind me. "She belong to you, Ronin?"

I twirl around, my face hot with embarrassment. And yes, there he is, in all his top-model splendor, except with actual clothes on this time.

Ronin looks at me with a satisfied grin. "That's right, Angie. This one belongs to me all right. And we'll be eating here, so just send Cindy back when she's got time."

And then he hooks my arm around his and leads me towards the back of the diner. "Now, princess, do you mind telling me how you got yourself to Cookie's when I left you locked in your tower?"

"You left me up there on purpose?"

"How else could I keep an eye on you while I went out for drinks? You're not twenty-one, right? No bars for the baby. But I see you are resourceful. I might have to keep the reins a little tighter on you than the others."

I scoff at his boldness as he pushes me to sit in a booth at the back of the diner. Who the hell does this guy think he is? "Look, Ronin, I'm not sure how all the details of this deal will shake out, but I'm just going to go ahead and make one thing clear right now. I'm not in the market for big brother, I can take care of myself, and if you try and lock me in the building again, I'm leaving for good. I don't take shit from any—"

"You all ready to order, Ronin?"

The waitress, Cindy I guess, is standing over us tapping her pen on her little order pad.

"Yeah," Ronin says, clearing his throat. "The usual for me, and bring one for her too, but make it well-done."

"Excuse me! I can order for myself. And I'd like—" I have no menu, so I make it up. "A grilled chicken salad."

The waitress eyes me, then bends down to write her ticket as she looks to Ronin for confirmation. What is up with that?

"She'll have my usual, well-done."

Cindy clicks her gum and walks off, ripping the order off the pad and clamping it up on one of those turn-style things for the cook in back.

"How dare you?"

"How dare I what?" He's grinning at me again and if he wasn't so damn irritating with his controlling bullshit, I might be tempted to gaze at him for a while. His eyes blaze with mischief, like I'm entertaining him or something, and then he leans back, kicks out his legs and pushes them against mine under the table. He drapes his arm over the back of the booth with a satisfied grin and my heart beats a little faster.

He's touching me.

I pull my leg back and he laughs. "Ah, yes, I forgot. Rook, the only model in the history of Antoine Chaput studios who refuses to be touched. You're gonna have to get over that. Real fast."

"How dare you order for me?" I reply, ignoring his flirt, or threat, or whatever the hell that comment just was. "I have no idea what your *usual* is, and who are you to tell me to eat it well-done anyway? I just wanted a salad."

I get nothing from him beyond that confident smile. We stare at each other for a few moments and he looks me straight in the eyes. Like he can see through me or something. I try to keep his gaze, but I lose the contest and look away first as my heart does a weird dance inside my chest.

"Relax, Rook. This place is famous for their burgers so I ordered you a burger. Well-done, because that's how most people eat their burgers. I like mine medium-rare, but I don't like the idea of you eating undercooked hamburger, so I got it well-done, OK? Do you want me to change the order? I will if you prefer medium or rare or whatever."

I look away, embarrassed. Did I just overreact? Or did he just play me?

There's no time to answer because a girl dressed up like a biker straight out of Sturgis saunters up to Ronin and plants herself next to him in the booth. She ignores me completely.

"Ronin, my love. Does this outfit scream STURGIS, or what?"

It's like she read my mind. A laugh bursts out before I can stop it and the wannabe biker chick shoots me a dirty look.

"Sorry," I mumble.

"We're not casting for STURGIS until TRAGIC is over, Lisa. You'll have to come back in a few weeks."

"Well, I can do TRAGIC, too! I'm tragic, right?"

"Ah, you are, sweetie. But Rook here is our new TRAGIC girl, sorry. That job is taken."

My eyebrows shoot up. "I am?"

Lisa jumps on my indecision. "She's not signed yet?"

"It doesn't matter, Lisa, Antoine and I chose her this afternoon during her test shoot. She's the girl we want." And then he looks over to me and smiles. But this time it's not cocky and bold. It's warm and seductive—a little crooked with a promise of something devious and a hint of dirty in it. Everything inside me goes warm in an instant. "So we'll do whatever it takes to keep her."

Lisa pouts and whines a little more but Ronin is looking straight at me the whole time. His gaze gets uncomfortable and I have to look away.

I take a deep breath and when I look up again, Lisa is gone and the food is here. Ronin helps Cindy with the plates and scoots my burger over towards me, says some flirty words to the waitress who looks exhausted and ready to go home, and then winks at me as he takes a bite of his food.

Chapter Nine

Ronin

This Rook is going to be a handful, I can tell. She's got a dark look to her, a look that says she's had some trouble recently. But she's not down, that's for sure. And her defenses are on high alert. Much too high for my comfort level. I'll have to work on that. If she doesn't trust me to order her food, then she's definitely not going to trust me to take care of her during a shoot.

And even though I told Lisa Rook is definitely the girl I want for TRAGIC, we won't get far if we can't touch her. *I* can't touch her, I correct myself. I'm the one who'll be touching her.

She has a good appetite once she settles in and starts eating, and that's a plus. I can only eat half of my burger, too many beers tonight, but Rook scarfs hers down and makes a decent dent in her French fries as well. I smile as she leans back in the booth. "Satisfied?" She blushes a bright pink and I have to stop myself from growling with desire. This girl does something to me and I'm not quite sure what to do about it.

"I was hungry," she explains. "I didn't eat all day."

"That's not good," I say, frowning at her. This might be an issue after all. "You want some pie? Cookie makes the best pies in town."

She laughs, as if this is absurd. "No, thanks. I've had enough."

I stand and hold out my hand to her. She looks at me funny but accepts it and I pull her to her feet and put my hand behind her back to direct her to the door.

"Don't we have to pay?"

"We have a tab, Rook. When you eat here you walk to the back booth, you order whatever you want and they bill us. No questions asked."

"Oh, then you take it out of our pay or something?"

I hold the door open for her and she murmurs a thank you as she passes through. I love her manners. She's a contradiction though, dark and defensive one minute, sweet and innocent the next. I'm not sure which side I prefer to be honest, I like them both at the moment. "No, this is just what we do for the models. We like you girls to look a certain way. Make sense?"

She looks over to me as we cross the street and make our way back to the studio. "I guess."

She has no idea what I'm talking about, and I'm really too tired to explain, so I just walk next to her in silence until we get to the door. "You can use my code for now, all right? It's 37351 I'll write it down for you when we get upstairs. It works for the terrace door too, so you're not a princess anymore."

She laughs at that and I have a sudden urge to put my hands all over her body, that's how much those little noises coming from her mouth turn me on. I can't even remember the last time a girl made me feel like that. Maybe never.

"Sorry for escaping, the hunger about drove me mad."

Oh shit. I feel bad. I'm such an asshole.

"But thanks for the burger. I really did like it."

We trudge up the four flights of stairs with just the noise of our footfalls to break the silence. Her little Converse sneakers are cute—bright red with little holes near the toes, like she's been wearing them since she was twelve and can't bear to give them up. I open the studio door and make sure it clicks closed behind us. "We've got the doors on a lock timer, so if you come in during business hours, it's always open, but after hours you need the code."

I open the terrace door for her and wait for her to walk through, then follow her out onto the terrace.

"This place is so beautiful, even in the moonlight."

I look around at it. I'm so used to living here I don't even notice the cherry trees anymore. "Yeah, Antoine spends a small fortune on gardeners every month. We shoot a lot of stuff out here though, so it's worth it I guess."

She looks longingly at the grass and flowering fruit trees. "I spent most of my life in the city and there were some pretty places, I mean every city has pretty places, right? But they never quite made up for the ugliness."

Something tells me she's not talking about Denver.

"There's a swing over there near the first tree." I take her arm and pull her along with me over to the trees. "Get on. I'll push you."

I half expect a little fight out of her, but she's a lot calmer than she was when I found her in the diner. I watched her come out of the alley, get nervous about a group of guys following her, and then overreact when another guy asked her a question. She was wound up tight when I showed up.

But now—I listen to her stifle down a laugh as she settles down on the old wooden swing—she's calm and soft.

I think I prefer her like this. I can do without the dark Rook, but this girl, the one who says thank you when I open the door for her and who giggles when I push her in the cherry tree swing—this girl is sexy. Rook has Lisa and her Sturgis outfit beat by a mile and all she's wearing is some ripped-up low-cut jeans and an oversized white t-shirt that shows zero cleavage.

Her long dark hair floats out behind her as she swings forward, and then whips against her back as she returns to me. I catch a glimpse of her bare neck every once in a while and I get the urge to kiss her there. *Shit, Ronin, what's wrong with you?* Models are not girlfriend material, I remind myself. They are the farthest thing from girlfriend material there is. I try not to date the models, I try not to even look at them.

But Rook isn't a model. She might be one next week when we start this campaign, but right now, she's just a girl.

And the only thing I know right now is that I want her.

"So Rook, tell me. Do you think you'll like modeling?"

"Yeah," she says, "I'll love it, as long as it pays me money. I just want a job, you know?"

She tilts her head back as she swings forward, making her whole body dip, and I imagine how she might look underneath me in bed—arching her back as I tickle her stomach with kisses. I snap out of the fantasy. "Do you have family here in Denver?"

"No."

That's all I get. *No.*

"Friends?"

"Nope."

Again, she offers nothing.

"So how did you get here?" I push.

"Fate." She laughs and jumps off the swing the next time it goes forward. She lands on her knees in the grass and then rolls down on her back. "That was fun, thank you." She gets to her feet and waits.

Despite her smile and her laugh, I recognize the move. She just ended the night.

"You're welcome. Want me to write the code down for you? So you can go get breakfast in the morning?"

"Yeah, sure," she says, already walking towards the garden studio. She punches in her code, which is all ones, so not a big deal, but she punches it in like she's lived here all year and not half a day. "Is there some paper and a pen in here? I haven't looked through everything yet."

"Yeah," I say. "In the top drawer next to the stove."

She shoots me a weird look, wondering how I know that probably, but I don't offer up an explanation and she simply hands the stuff over and I write down my code. "The doors are off hours all weekend, so you have to use the code at all times. OK?"

She nods. "Thanks."

Aaaaand… that's it. She's shut me down.

I take the hint and move towards the door. "OK, I guess I'll see you around tomorrow?"

She holds the door as I stand there waiting for an answer. "Sure."

I sigh and step out, feeling a little hurt as the door

quickly closes behind me.

Chapter Ten

I lean my body back against the door after I force myself to close it on Ronin's face. It was so difficult to end this night but I'm not ready to get close to anyone, especially a guy like Ronin. He's dangerous, I can tell. He's some kind of supermodel, he runs the girls, whatever that means, and he's hot as fucking hell.

I giggle at my private swooning.

But it's true. My heart is still racing and it's not all because he scares me either. He does scare me though. I'm afraid of just about everything he represents. I mean let's be honest, all the best-looking guys cheat. That's a given. They know they look good, they probably spend all their time at the gym trying to maintain those bodies, and they only want one thing. But they want that one thing from as many girls as they can get, not just one thing from one girl. Because if I could find me a hot guy who only wanted that one thing from just me, I might think about it.

But seriously—Ronin is not that guy. He's practically

got himself a harem of models that he claims like a caveman. Hell, even Elise told me to tell the diner I belonged to Ronin.

It's degrading.

And that whole ordering for me thing? I'm still confused about that. Because we both know it started out as a challenge, to see how far I'd let him walk all over me. But then he turned it on me with his logic and made me feel stupid for putting up a fight.

I huff out a breath and walk back to the bedroom and shuffle through my backpack to find my toothbrush. Everything I own is contained in this bag. And it's not much. Two pairs of jeans, besides the ones I'm wearing. And four more t-shirts. I don't even have underwear, because if you can believe this, someone at the shelter pilfered through my stuff and stole it all. They didn't just steal the underwear, that would be sick. They took all my clothes. So I had to get these all from the thrift store down the street from the shelter last week.

I grab what few toiletries I have and pull out a drawer to stash them away.

But the drawer is filled with stuff. Girl stuff. Make-up, lotion, nail polish. All sorts of things I'd love to buy on a regular basis but have had to go without for the past few months.

I sigh with satisfaction and then start to brush my teeth.

Rook, your luck has changed. This is a huge break. Last night I was holding a knife to my chest, ready to cut the pervert in the cot next to me if he tried to touch me again, and tonight I'm living—*living*—in a rooftop garden apartment on the trendy side of town. Is life weird or what?

It is weird, but I try not to think about it too much

because if life can change for the better this fast, then it can change for the worse as well. I remember the money Elise gave me this afternoon and dash back to the bedroom to pull it out from under the mattress. I guess it's overkill to stash money in my own apartment that I live in by myself—this makes me privately squeal—but I can't help it.

Plus, I remind myself that I am making a list of why Ronin is not the guy for me, no matter how fast my heart thumps when he's near. That whole *I'll order for you* thing is cute the first time they do it, maybe. It's not for me, but if I was another girl, it might be cute. But in my mind, that shit is a red flag. Flying high out above his head. It says *I want to control you.*

And I'm not into that at all. Hell, I barely escaped the last boyfriend with my life, there's no way I'm getting involved with another guy who thinks he can tell me what to do.

And Ronin is flirting with the very edge of my boundary in that area.

I spit out the toothpaste and rinse out my mouth, then start the bath water and push the plug in the drain of the massive claw-foot tub. Maybe… yes! Bubbles under the vanity! I dump in a lot, far more than I need, but who cares. It's my tub and these are my bubbles! I can use as many as I want.

I worry about getting so excited about all this stuff, and getting used to it most of all. It sucks when you're used to something nice and then you lose it, but if you never have it in the first place, then you don't have to worry about losing it. Right?

That's how I think. And it works for me. Keeps my expectations low-key and my bullshit detector on high alert.

I peel off the clothes and slip into the hot water and enjoy how the bubbles feel as they float over my body.

I think I might be happy.

Maybe.

The last time I was happy I was fifteen.

And that is very sad. But tonight is not a night to be sad. Tonight is a night to have a private celebration that I made it. I'm OK. My eyes are not black and my body is not bruised. I'm OK. I'm safe.

And that asshole is one thousand miles away.

I smirk at this. *Asshole.*

I dunk my head under and shake my hair, then pop back up and relax.

Yeah, that Ronin. He's one cute guy and all. But he's not for me. Even if he is tall and has those amazing blue eyes. I bet if we had babies our kids would totally have the most cornflower blue eyes ever. And dark raven hair. Oh God, we'd make little model babies. They'd need agents at birth.

I am crazy!

Thinking about his little blue-eyed babies. It's fun, in a sixth-grade fangirl kind of way. But I'd rather think about this TRAGIC contract to be honest. And the money that might come with it. I'm not sure how much it might pay or what it involves, but I'm definitely in. Antoine and Elise seem nice. At the very least, they seem on the up and up. So I think I will trust them. And anyway, Elise said I could shampoo hair for a job, so even if the TRAGIC contract doesn't pan out, I still have an apartment and a job.

For a little while anyway.

Ugh. The fear of losing good things creeps back in. I like this new life. I could get used to this very fast and I've never had anything that was even close to being this beautiful as far as apartments go. But Elise gave me the secret. She said keep your mouth shut and do what you're told. So, if that's all it takes to make Antoine happy with me, I can do that. I'll definitely do that.

I pull the plug with my toes and dip under one last time to wet my hair again. I'll wash when I wake up, but right now all I want to do is try out my new mattress. I giggle again as I get out of the tub, wrap a ridiculously extravagant towel around my body, and stumble over to the bed. I only mean to lie down for a second, but once my head hits the pillow, the thought of getting back up to change is just too much.

I slip into sleep already dreaming about Ronin pushing me on the cherry tree swing.

Chapter Eleven

Ronin

I spend the next hour on my own terrace that overlooks the large one down below, just watching the shadows move across her apartment. I can't see anything, so I don't think this is stalking or weird. I just want to see if she's OK. And to make sure she doesn't try to leave again.

Whatever. I want to catch a glimpse of her.

But I don't because the curtains, while sheer, are not really see-though. I see a shadow come and go, like she was in the bathroom for a while with the door open, because the light stays the same. And then no movement.

And the lights stay on.

I have an overwhelming need to find out why she has the lights on and I have to stop myself from going down there and asking her. Is she afraid of the dark? Did she slip and fall and knock herself out? Did she forget to turn them off and fell asleep?

I have to force myself to go back inside, undress, and lie down in the darkness.

But I cannot get her out of my mind.

She's got a past, that much is evident. And it's not a good one from the way she runs from it. But I want to know. If she signs the TRAGIC contract we'll get her social security information and maybe I'll run a background check.

That's devious. Maybe even stalkerish. But if she's an employee, it's my duty. I'd run a check on any new girl who came to us out of nowhere. Which has never happened before. Antoine only takes referrals. Rook not only appeared out of nowhere, she has no agency, no book, and no interest in talking about her past. Bolt was the word Elise used. She might take her money and *bolt* if we don't tread carefully.

So if the shampoo job is a way to keep her, I'll make sure she's trained by Monday. That way we can keep her busy all day, do her second shoot after hours, and then explain the contract and get her to sign it that night.

At dinner maybe. Yeah, Elise and Antoine can make us dinner.

Us?

Shit, I really need to stop thinking of her like this.

This sounds like a plan and when I have a plan, I'm happy. My mind settles down from the day's activities, and I think about her huddled form in the hallway after watching Clare storm out. She was scared. I make a mental note not to scare her. Ever. And then fall asleep dreaming about pushing Rook in the cherry tree swing.

I wake up in the morning—well, after I reach over and check my phone, I realize it's late afternoon. And the second thing I do is pop up out of bed and start thinking about Rook. I wander out to the terrace to see if the lights are still on, but I can't tell. The whole building is awash with golden light from the afternoon sun.

I jump in the shower real fast, pull on some pants, and then head out the door barefoot and shirtless. I skip down the stairs and head straight to the garden apartment. When I get there I can plainly tell that the lights are still on. I cup my hands around my eyes and peek in through the front door window, but I can't see her on the bed, even though I have a straight line-of-sight from this door to that room.

I knock.

And wait.

And knock. And peer in again.

And then punch in the code to unlock the door.

"Rook?" Maybe she left? "Rook?" I walk back to the bedroom and stop short, my breath caught in my lungs.

She's sprawled out naked on her bed, the covers draped around her body, twined around her legs to cover her ass, and one breast is visible as she turns with a moan.

"Rook?"

She bolts upright and all her covers slip down her chest, baring herself to me. "What the hell?"

Her body is perfect. Flawless. Her skin glows in the light that flows into the western-facing window. She's still not fully awake yet and I take advantage of her indecisive moment to study her further. Her raven-dark hair is tousled around her face in waves and she rubs her eyes, breathing hard for a moment from the surprise.

There is no way in hell I'm leaving here without touching this girl. I tug her to her feet and smile as she realizes just how exposed she is and frantically makes a grab for the sheet. She looks up at me, or tries to, because her eyes get stuck on my own bare chest. I grin a little internally that I can shake her up like that. Eventually she pulls her eyes from my body and finds my eyes.

"What are you doing?"

Her voice is deep and throaty and I can't contain the chill she sends down my arms. I reach for her hair and she pulls away, gasping a little. "Shhhh. I won't hurt you, Rook." I have her full attention as my hand gathers the hair and pulls it down over her right breast, which is now hidden under the sheet. She relaxes under my touch and I get a wave of courage so I repeat the action, draping her long hair over her left breast.

And then I stop.

We stop.

The whole world stops.

And there is nothing but breathing, heavy with expectation.

"You're beautiful," I whisper as I take her hand and pull it down to her side. She whimpers a little and immediately grabs for the sheet with the other hand. "Trust me," I say. And then I tug on the sheet so that it slips down her stomach and falls to the floor. Her breasts are covered by her tresses, which tumble down her front like a waterfall. "Do you trust me?"

She shakes her head no and looks down.

I brush a finger down her front, lightly dragging it through the hair that covers her nipple, making her bite her lip and let out a whimper. Her eyes dart around the room, looking everywhere but at my face.

"Look at me, Rook," I command more harshly than I should.

I can tell she wants to put up a fight, but her will collapses under my pressure and she meets my gaze and then my smile allows her to relax.

"Why are you doing this?" she asks softly.

I gather some hair and drag it over her right shoulder so that it falls down her back and exposes her breast at the same time. Only the city lights streaming through the large window leave her bare. Just the one half of her body is illuminated, the rest is safe in the shadows.

I reach in my pocket and pull out my phone. "What do we do here, Rook? In this studio?"

Her eyes never leave mine. "Take pictures."

My phone makes a camera shutter sound.

"We're going to take a lot of pictures of you." I turn the phone around so she can see the picture. It's not the best, it's a phone camera after all, and the light is bad. But it tells her what she needs to know.

"It's pretty," she says, smiling at her first artistic portrait.

"Yes," I say, turning it back so I can look at it. It's fucking gorgeous. "And even though you're standing here in front of me with no clothes on, and even though everyone who sees this picture will instinctively know that you had no clothes on when I took it, they will only see what I allow them to see through the frame of this lens."

She bends down and pulls the sheet back up to cover herself. "You broke into my apartment to teach me a lesson?"

I love her response, it tells me two things: She's not a pushover and she's game for this contract.

"No, I came to see if you were OK. No, that's not true either. I came because I haven't stopped—" My phone vibrates and I lose track of my words. I look down at it and read the text.

"Shit, I gotta go. I'll bring back dinner if you want." I look back at her as I leave the bedroom and catch her shrugging. "Just give me a couple hours," I call out behind me as I leave.

I grab a shirt and some shoes from my apartment and stare at the image of Rook on my phone all the way down to the parking garage. When I get to my truck I realize the real reason I went into her apartment. I don't want to ruin this girl but I'm not sure I can stop it now.

Chapter Twelve

Holy shit!

Not only is this Ronin guy able to make all my girly bits shudder, he's got a flair for the dramatic as well. I can still feel his fingertips as they tracked down my breast. And I just stood there and let him do it!

What the fuck is wrong with me?

I laugh. This guy, that's what's wrong with me.

I need air, so I wrap the sheet around me and go out on the terrace. The spring breeze is nice and cool and my head begins to clear almost immediately. I peek over the wall and watch the people down below. It's not that crowded since it's still early evening. The sidewalks are mostly filled with families grabbing dinner. Something I very badly want to do as well.

A large black truck appears from under the building and I catch a bit of music leaking out from the cab. I bet that's Ronin's truck and I bet that text was from a girl. He'll be back with dinner my ass. I sigh and go back inside and start the shower. This tub is cool for baths, but as far as the shower goes, it sucks. There's like one of those kits they use to turn claw-foot tubs into showers, which means I have to stand there and use a hand-held sprayer every time I want to rinse.

"Oh, Rook," I say out loud as the bubbles stream down my body. "Last week you were showering in a homeless shelter twice a week if you were lucky. And now you're all high-and-mighty about using a hand-held sprayer?"

Yeah, getting used to things fast.

This is not good. I've been here two days and I'm being sucked up into this strange life of models and photographers and weird guys named after rogue Japanese killers who think they can order food for you and strip you naked after they break into your apartment.

I finish up in the shower and wrap the towel around me, anxious to get back to the bedroom. My hand slips under the mattress to the money Elise gave me yesterday. I haven't spent any of it and I won't, either. I'm saving this money, every bit they give me here, I'm saving it all up. Because if there's one thing in life I can count on, it's that eventually, no matter how freaking nice that rug is under your feet, someone always pulls it out from under you eventually.

I pull my jeans and t-shirt on and slip back out the front door to make my way into the studio kitchen. There's not much in there, just a fruit basket, some beer in the fridge, and a few frozen dinners in the freezer that have names on little sticky notes attached to them.

Apparently stealing someone's frozen skinny meal is verboten in this place.

I have no idea what goes on in a photography studio, or how models act, or what they eat, or how they stay so skinny or what happens if they get fat.

But I can take a good guess.

I'm thin because I was born this way. I'm tall because I was born this way. I'm not all that smart, I mean I'm of average intelligence I suppose, but I can't do much with math. And I don't pretend that I can understand politics or current events or scientific studies that tell me to stop blow-drying my hair or talking on a cell phone. Pretty much everything I know I learned from a movie. I'm crazy about movies and if I was pushed to describe my dream life, it wouldn't be modeling. My dream has always been to go to film school and make cool movies. Deep movies that have so many layers to them, people have to watch them a dozen times to get all the little inside jokes and nuances.

As a girl growing up in America you'd think I had it all. I mean, they fill you up with that we're-all-equal bullshit your whole life. *You can grow up to be anything*, my foster parents used to tell me. Right before they sent me back into the system, most of the time. But what they never mention is that dreams require money to fulfill.

They should just tell you this at the get-go if you ask me. Just state the facts and forget the equality crap. Because the facts are the facts. If someone had sat me down in the first grade and drilled it into my head that life is difficult, more difficult than I could ever imagine, and that success is neither guaranteed nor probable, and if they'd have followed that up with a step-by-step approach on how to get past all the pitfalls I might encounter along the way… well, I might not have tasted the poisoned honey my ex was selling when he found me, lost and desperate after running away from the tenth or twelfth foster home, and greedily accepted it as tasty.

Downright delicious, even.

They do us no favors, talking us up about women

astronauts and lawyers and whatever. Because the cold hard reality is that none of those things apply to you when you're poor.

Unless you've got someone looking out for you—and most girls have this in their parents, but not everyone has parents and even fewer have good parents—you're screwed unless you figure it out yourself. And in my case, I did figure it out, but I took the long road to get here, that's for sure.

I have very few assets. But the ones I have I plan on using to my full advantage. I'm thin, I'm tall, I have long legs, blue eyes, and black hair. My tits are bigger than most models I've seen, but they're not porn-star material. I have straight teeth, a bright white smile and well-defined cheekbones.

I might not have much, but I have this. I have looks. I have The Look, if these people aren't blowing smoke up my ass. I have what they want. So I'm not interested in Ronin's games or Elise's attempts at big sisterhood, or the cushy life they're giving me here.

Beauty is fleeting. I know someone important said that, but I have no idea who it was. I just know it's true. So I'm gonna grab this second chance with everything I've got and I'm gonna ride this wave until it spits me back out on the beach of bullshit.

Because I know better now.

I've seen what being poor and stupid and scared does to you. I looked at it in the mirror and I'm never going back there. And maybe Ronin is a nice guy, maybe he's nothing like my ex, but I can't take the chance. I have my own dreams and Antoine Chaput's photography studio is just one more stop along the way to get to the place in life where *I* want to be.

I grab my phone and two twenties from under my

mattress. I have no intention of spending them, but it's stupid to leave home without a phone and money, so I'm not about to do that. And I leave the safety and seclusion of the studio and go back out in to the real world to get my own dinner.

No boys bother me this time.

The words don't get stuck in my throat when I meet the hostess in Cookie's. I say "I belong to Ronin" because I have to. This is what I do to get by for now. I order a salad because while I might've been born thin, eating hamburgers every night is a guaranteed way to pack on the pounds and when your body is your money maker, you don't screw yourself over like that.

I eat and watch people and when the waitress comes by to check on me I order some scrambled eggs and bacon to take home and stick in the fridge for breakfast.

When the order's ready I take my free food and walk back to the studio and crawl in bed, thankful that I have somewhere to sleep, a bit of food to hold me over, and a general feeling of secure well-being, even if it is only temporary.

Ronin Flynn never shows up with dinner and instead of making me angry, this makes me happy.

Because I had him pegged right from the start. Ronin is a player, a user, and a control freak. And I want absolutely nothing to do with him. I'm here to make money and that's all.

Chapter Thirteen

I wake slowly in the morning. I can hear the birds singing and recall leaving the door open to get some air flow through the screen door last night when I came home from the diner. It smells like spring. The air is cool and the gentle breeze travels all the way down the hallway to my bedroom and flutters the clean white sheets.

I think this is the best moment of my life.

Like ever.

I've never had my own apartment, I've never had my own bed, and I've never woken up in such a nice place two days in a row. I roll over and sigh, content. The sheets are wrapped around my body and it feels good. They are expensive sheets, I think. They are soft. Softer than anything I've ever slept on before.

My eyes open and I spy my pack on the floor. All my clothes are dirty and I really need to do laundry. This place even has a washer and dryer and I almost giggle aloud at this thought. No laundromats for me. For now anyway.

I push that moment of caution away because what's the point of having all this good stuff if I can't enjoy it while it lasts?

My legs swing out of the bed and I gather up all my clothes and stick them in the stackable washer in the closet just off the bedroom. The breeze caresses my naked limbs and gives me the chills, but I enjoy it. The goose bumps travel up my arms and spread out to my whole body. I shiver for a second and then head to the kitchen.

And stop dead in the living room.

Ronin fucking Flynn is sleeping on the couch.

What is he doing here? My eyes track to the front door and I suppose it's my fault, I left it open. There's nothing but a screen door between this apartment and the terrace. My gaze wanders back to the sleeping man. He's lying on his stomach, his one arm tucked underneath him, the other falling over the edge of the cushion, and he's shirtless.

And then I realize I'm naked.

"Shit!"

He stirs and I make a break for the bedroom. It's one thing to let him see me naked half hidden in darkness and quite another to be fully illuminated by the bright morning sunshine. I wrangle the sheet around my body and then head back to the living room, wistfully looking at the washer that contains every single article of clothing I own.

"Ronin!" I say loudly.

Nothing except a half-muffled snore from him. Lord, this man has the most perfectly chiseled and muscular back I've ever seen. Both hands pull up and go under his face, like he's blocking out the sunlight, and this gives me the perfect opportunity to study his flexing biceps. The muscles are thick and hard-looking near his shoulders. They curve down, dip into a little valley, and then climb once again.

I lean down and smell him.

"Why are you sniffing me?" he asks groggily.

"Uh—" *Because you smell delicious,* the inner Rook says. But luckily the outer Rook says, "I'm checking to see if you're drunk. Why are you sleeping on my couch?"

He peeks up, opening one eye in my direction, squints, and then croaks out some words. "I love your outfit." He grins, winks, and then drops his head back down into his arms.

"Are you leaving?" I ask, frustrated and confused at the same time. "I mean, why are you here?"

"I told you I'd come back with dinner. But when I got here, the lights were on and you were in bed. I only sat down for a second to think up a rational excuse to wake you up, but I guess I fell asleep." He raises his head again, grins sheepishly, and then rolls over on his back, tucks his hands behind his neck, and flashes his perfect body at me as he closes his eyes, probably confident that I'll be checking him out.

I do check him out. It's quite hard not to notice that he's got the perfect six-pack abs and that absolutely adorable fuzzy happy trail you see on a shirtless designer jeans model. Hmmmm… maybe he *is* that model? "You have no shirt on."

Yes, after all that gawking, I finally manage the obvious.

He opens the one eye to look at me again. "Neither do you."

"I just put all my clothes in the washer. If I had known you were out here, I'd have saved an outfit to wear."

"Oh," he says, sitting up suddenly. "So you have to be naked until the clothes are finished?" He stands and we are only inches apart. He is so close I can feel the heat coming off his body. His hands find my hips under the bunched-up sheet and he sways me a little. "I'm still tired. Come with me." And then he takes my hand, leaving me scrambling to make up for the loss of one limb holding up my sheet, and tugs me back to the bedroom.

"Wait!" I say, resisting before we walk through the doorway. "What're you doing?"

"Going back to bed, Rook. It's early. Way too early to get up and worry about clothes." He tugs me to the bed and sits down. "Sleep next to me for a few more hours."

Holy crap. What do I say to that? "Uh," is all that comes out. He takes my indecision as a signal, which it is, if I'm being honest. Regardless of all those feminist she-nis thoughts I had last night lying here alone, this morning his self-serving idea sounds like a well-thought-out plan. So he pulls me the rest of the way down and I'm sitting next to his prone body.

"Lie down, come on. I won't bother you, I promise. Let's sleep for a little longer."

I give in. I'm weak, what can I say? He's hot, and not just in the looks department, he's got a heat radiating off his body that is calling me. It wants to wrap me up and it's been a while since I had that kind of affection, so I sink into the bed next to him and his arms open and then settle against my stomach.

I close my eyes. Because this feels good. This feels better than good actually, this feels perfect. He tucks his face down into my hair and takes a deep breath.

I smile because he just sniffed me.

"I'm just checking to see if you're drunk, ma'am."

I giggle a little.

"And if I wasn't so tired, I'd check you for drugs as well. Pat you down until I found your hidden stash."

"I'm naked, remember?"

"Awwww, come on, Rook! I'm trying not to think about that. Be good now, or I'll break my promise and bother you all up. Make you all bothered..." His voice trails off, already giving in to the call of sleep.

My entire body releases four years of tension and fear. And I snuggle against his chest.

And fall asleep thinking this is what people mean when they say they are content.

Chapter Fourteen

When I wake I'm alone, but I can hear the TV out in the living room blaring a baseball game, so I know I'm not really alone. I smile at this. He's still here, watching baseball in the living room. Like he belongs here.

Maybe he does belong here?

Rook, stop it. He's a player, he's a user, and he's probably got a million girls strung out all over this city. That's why he left last night and that's why he came back so late. And then you went and let him sleep in your bed and act like he's your boyfriend.

This has got to stop.

I roll off the bed, still clutching my sheet to my body, then pad over to the laundry closet in the hallway.

"I already took care of it." Ronin calls out.

"Took care of what?" I ask, peeking around the corner to see him. He's kicking back on the couch, feeding himself peanuts and drinking a beer. "Sheesh, comfortable much?"

"You know what the best part of living next to the baseball stadium is, Rook?" he asks, ignoring my snarky remark.

I shrug and simultaneously listen to the *Charge!* organ music on the TV and the fans outside in the stadium as they go wild.

He points to the bag of peanuts in his hand. "Baseball park peanuts at home." He grins a huge, wide-eyed, baseball-is-awesome-and-so-are-peanuts grin.

"You went over there to get peanuts?"

"No." He shakes his head. "I got a guy."

I laugh. "What? You have a peanut guy? Like a peanut dealer, who stands on the corner and sells peanuts from the curb as you drive by?"

"Nah, that's stupid. He delivers them to the freaking door. Anyway," he says, waving a hand at me. "I folded your laundry for you and do you know what I found out?"

"What?" I ask, shaking my head.

"That you do not own any panties."

My whole face goes hot. "*What?*"

"Panties, Rook," he says, pointing to the laundry closet with his bag of stadium peanuts. "I folded your seven articles of clothing over there so that when you woke up you'd have something to wear besides that sheet, and I found no undergarments."

I open the closet and there are my seven articles of clothing sitting on top of the stackable washer lid. Folded. "Uh…"

When I turn Ronin is standing next to me taking a swig of beer. He swallows and grins. "I can help you out with that, if you'd like."

"I'm lost. Are we talking about getting me panties, or taking them off me?"

He laughs. "Both, I think. Come on," he says, taking my hand and setting his beer down on the coffee table as we walk by. He pulls me outside and the only thing I smell is cherry blossoms. Every single cherry tree is filled with flowers, so many flowers every bough bends under the weight. It creates a heaviness that transfers across the terrace and pulls me into the scenery. Ronin catches my gaze and stops for a moment. "We're gonna take pictures of you out here tomorrow. It will be perfect, don't you think?"

I stare at the trees a few more moments and then mutter, "They're so beautiful I can barely stand to look at them."

"I know the feeling." His boyish charms are gone now as he looks down on me with a hunger I haven't seen on a man's face in a very long time. "And a picture of you surrounded by those blossoms will be enough to make a guy shed a tear over the perfection of it all."

I wait for the joke but it never comes. He just stares at me for a few more seconds and then squeezes my hand and pulls me into the studio.

"Where are we going? I have no clothes on!"

"Exactly," he comes back with. We enter a small hallway near the stairs and walk to the end of it and turn a corner to find a double door. It has a keypad and Ronin punches in his code, which I notice is the same one that opens the outside doors. The same one he gave me the first day I met him.

"That code of yours works a lot of stuff around here. You should maybe not hand it out to just anyone."

"I didn't." He grins and pushes against the frosted glass until the doors begin to open automatically. He waves me into the room and then flicks on the lights.

I gasp.

"Welcome to the Chaput Studios wardrobe and dressing room. You may choose anything you want from this side of the closet." He points to the largest area where racks are overflowing with clothes. There must be thousands of outfits here. "Those over there," his gaze goes to the smaller section, "are for the next week's shoot. And these right here," he says, pointing to a large chest of thin drawers, "are undergarments. These are all new, so take what you want."

"Am I allowed?" I ask, stunned.

"Allowed what?"

"To take this stuff."

"I just said you could."

"But won't Antoine or Elise get mad that I'm pilfering your stuff?"

"I run the girls, Rook. That means I run the closet too. This is like my little kingdom."

I laugh again. Shit, this guy has me laughing like an idiot this morning. "You're the King of the Closet?"

He bows. "The one and only."

"And you have spare panties for *me*?"

"Just shut up and pick some clothes, you goof."

"I don't know where to start, honestly. I've not had a lot of opportunities to shop."

He looks over at me as I take seat on a long bench in the middle of the room. His expression is a little sad. "I'm not going to ask, because I know you've got things you're not about to reveal to me, not after three days anyway. But I'd just like you to know, that is not right. Whatever you've been through, whatever it was that made you so… sad. I'd just like to say you deserve better."

I swallow down some old hurt and mumble out a, "Thank you."

Chapter Fifteen

Ronin

"You're welcome, but you're definitely getting clothes today. This closet is bursting with shit so I'll tell you what, you look through the bras and panties and I'll bring you clothes. I have excellent taste anyway."

I go off to find her something comfortable. I pass by the sexy stuff, then grab a pretty nightie just in case, and continue on and find the casual wear.

Rook's clothes aren't that bad. I mean, she looks hot as hell to me. I don't look at that shit at all. Now her body, that's something else. I look at her body. But I work with girls every day. Beautiful girls. The most beautiful girls in the world, actually. And I know that when they wear pretty things, they feel pretty.

So I get Rook just about every pretty thing I can find, whether she needs it or not. I flip through the rack of jeans for some soft ones and grab several pairs. She must like jeans because that's the only thing I've seen her in, and besides, I like her in jeans and I'm the one choosing. If she doesn't like what I get, she can come shop for herself.

I grab some t-shirts like she's been wearing, but also some other stuff. Frilly things, tailored things, a few skirts, some shorts, tank tops, I grab all of it.

I catch myself grinning as I round the corner and come out of the circular closet behind her. "Here you go."

She spins around from the drawer of underwear, startled, like I scared the ever-loving shit out of her. And it hits me. Something very bad happened to this girl, and it wasn't that long ago from the way she acts.

Slow down, Ronin.

"Here, try these on."

She takes the handful of clothes out of my arms and I back away. "I'll be out in the studio if you need anything, OK?"

To my surprise she comments to me on everything I brought, yelling out as she tries them on one at a time.

"How'd you know what size jeans I wear?"

We only have three sizes, and if she wasn't one of those sizes, she wouldn't have gotten past the door. She's not all bones like some girls, so the small size is out, and she's bigger up top than any of the models I've seen come through here, so I figure the larger of the three sizes is safe.

I say none of this out loud, I ignore that question altogether. That's a trap if ever there was one.

"Nice try with the nightie!"

Now this topic is safe. "I picked it because it's blue and I thought to myself, Ronin, that girl out there has the prettiest blue eyes, wouldn't she look spectacular in this little slip of see-through fabric that is a shade or two lighter."

She walks out of the dressing room as the last few

words are coming out of my mouth.

Wearing the nightie.

I'm speechless and I'm pretty fucking sure my mouth is hanging open.

"I thought since you went to the trouble and put all that thought into it, you at least deserved to see it on."

"You are very bad, Rook. Very, very bad."

She laughs all the way up to her eyes and my heart is filled with… something. Something weird. Heat flushes through my body and I almost lose my train of thought when she begins to turn away.

"Hey!" I call. "Come back here a minute, you distracted me and I missed some parts."

To my surprise she turns back around and stands there, her hip jutting out, one hand practically caressing the wall and an unreadable expression on her face.

She's not flaunting it, not modeling, or twirling around to hide her embarrassment. She just stands there and allows me to look at her. I almost feel guilty as my eyes travel down her body and then stop at the bottom and make their way up again. Half of her long black hair is flowing over one shoulder, but the rest of it peeks out from behind her back like a cape. "Miss Walsh," I whisper, "you've wiped my mind of everything right now."

I walk up to her and she averts her eyes but when I get closer she fights hard to meet my gaze. "I'm glad you're here," I tell her honestly. I want to take her face in my hands and kiss her so bad, but I make myself behave. "I hope you understand that. I'm a flirt and I joke a lot but—" I lose my train of thought as she starts breathing a little harder, making her chest rise and fall under the very sheer pale blue fabric that barely covers her breasts. "—but you *stun* me."

I finally find her face again and she's watching me closely, leaning in a little maybe—like she wants me to kiss her.

But then the moment passes and she turns away slowly. I watch her body move down the short hallway until she rounds the corner and starts talking again. "You're an excellent shopper, Ronin. I think I'll keep them all, but only if you take it out of my check." She comes back out a few minutes later dressed in a t-shirt and some jeans, holding the huge pile of clothes in her arms. On top is the sheer blue nightie.

"You're keeping the nightie?" is all I manage to say.

And then we both laugh because I am such a fucking pig.

"Yes, thank you for picking it out. I agree, it really makes my eyes look spectacular."

"Right," I breathe. "Your eyes."

"So you'll take this out of my check, right?"

"No."

"What do you mean, no?"

"No, I'm not taking the clothes out of your check. It's like the food, Rook. It comes with."

"Do you give all the girls free clothes?"

"No, but I would if they needed it."

"So I need it?"

"Don't you?" I see where this is going and a smarter guy would back off, but she's just being dumb.

"I don't really. I'm fine with the clothes I was wearing, it was you—"

"OK, whatever. I'll tell Elise to bill you for the clothes. Make you happy?"

She nods and I take the clothes from her arms and we walk across the terrace to her apartment. When we get inside I dump all her stuff on the bed and wait.

It's an awkward moment. Does she want me to leave? Stay? "Do you want to go get some lunch?"

"Um…"

"Before we train for tomorrow?" I stick that in to throw a wrench into her I'm-trying-to-get-rid-of-you plan, because I can see it coming.

"Train for tomorrow?"

"Yeah, I told Elise I'd train you at the shampoo station before she got back, you know, so she could relax on her romantic weekend getaway with Antoine. It's their anniversary. Well, sorta. They're not married, but they still call their first date their anniversary."

I'm fucking babbling.

"I need to train on the *shampoo station*?" is all she comes back with.

"Yeah, you know—the whole hot and cold water thing, shampoo versus conditioner. Detangler…"

I'm dying here.

"If you say so, Ronin. But I'm going to take a shower so why don't I meet you at the *shampoo station* in an hour and we'll talk about food afterward?"

Chapter Sixteen

Even though I should be thrilled at scoring a whole armful of designer clothes from the closet of Antoine Chaput's studio, I'm irritated as I wrestle with the stupid hand-held shower head thingy that won't let me relax and enjoy hot water at the same time. And Ronin. *Train on the shampoo station.* What kind of stupid way to spend a Sunday is that? I mean I get it, everything in my life is tentative right now, so I could do a lot worse than standing around listening to control-freak Ronin babble on about how to use the hot and cold water spigot.

I blow out a breath of air and rinse myself one last time and then give up on the shower being something fun. Next time I'll just take a bath, at least I can relax in a bath.

Who needs clean hair anyway?

Shampoo station training my ass.

I shake it off and go back into my room where all my new-to-me clothes are piled up on the bed. It is pretty cool that I got all this stuff though. I'll probably regret it when the bill comes, but that worry is for another day. Right now, I'm in underwear heaven. I fish out the prettiest panties I found and slip them on. They are black with little pink ribbons threaded through the butt and have tiny pink bows that accentuate each of my hipbones.

The jeans I wore out of the dressing room were perfect so I put those back on, and then wrangle my girls into the matching black and pink bra and add a black tank top to the ensemble. I look in the mirror. My hair is a bit of a mess and might even still have soap in it due to lack of proper rinsing, plus I have no make-up on to boot. But even so, this is the prettiest I've looked in years. Maybe ever.

I brush my teeth and then gloss up my lips with some brand new peach-tasting stuff I found in the make-up drawer. Imagine—three days of proper care and feeding can make up for four years of neglect and punishment.

It's amazing how little we humans really need to thrive and it blows my mind that a matching bra and panty set, coupled with the perfect pair of jeans, can lift my spirits up so high, it leaves me dizzy.

I sigh.

This is a lucky break. A total lucky break.

And even though I'm pretty sure I can handle the hot and cold water at the shampoo station, I'm going to be sweet and smile for Ronin as he explains these things to me like I'm an idiot. I can do that. And then I can ditch him and eat my leftover breakfast from Cookie's and spend a nice quiet evening watching TV alone.

Ahhhhhh… I let out a nice long breath and smile. I almost feel normal.

I slip my feet into my old Converse sneakers and head to the studio. Totally ready for shampoo station training. The weather outside is so perfect and the concrete is a bit damp, like it rained last night. I didn't hear any rain, but I was pretty dead to the world. The sweet scent of cherry blossoms wafts in the crosswind and even though there are all sorts of cars and people making noise and commotion down on the street, these trees cancel it all out. They make me feel like I'm walking across an orchard out in the country.

Inside the studio is bright and cheery and when I round the corner into the salon, Ronin's mood seems to match the atmosphere of the room. "Nice," he says.

I raise my eyebrows at him. Did he just use a player word on me? Ugh… how can such a good-looking guy be so irritating? "OK, I'm ready. Lay it on me, please explain all the technical details of how the hot and cold water handles work."

He grins. "You think it's easy, don't you? That shampooing doesn't require skill."

"Oh, I'm sure it does, but am I buying your whole I'm-an-expert-in-shampooing-stations act? No. But proceed. Teach me all I need to know about sinks."

"I think you've misunderstood, Rook. I'm not here to teach you how to use the sink. I'm going to teach you how to give a great shampoo."

I laugh. "OK, I'll ignore the fact that you specifically said hot and cold water and detangler earlier, but I've been shampooing my own rather lengthy, high-maintenance hair for a while now. I'm pretty sure I can handle it."

"But have you ever shampooed a man's hair? Huh? Because we have male models who need a shampoo here and Elise usually does her own shampoos. She's quite good at it, I hear, so they will be expecting the same treatment from you."

Is he for real? I look for the smirk that says he's

joking but I can't find it. "O-kaaaaaay," I say, drawing out the last syllable.

"So I'm going to show you how to give a Chaput Studios-worthy shampoo and then I'll test you and see if you've got it down."

"Test me how?"

"You can do me after I do you."

Again I look for the grin that will let me know he's playing around, but there is no hint of innuendo there. He seems serious. I frown. "We're going to shampoo each other's hair? Like a Gidget sleepover from the Sixties?"

This cracks his facade for a moment and he squints his eyes at me. "A what?"

"*Please*," I beg in an exaggerated manner, "do not tell me you're ignorant of Gidget? I might have to walk out."

"Do you buy it in the App Store?" he asks innocently.

A laugh puffs out through my cheeks and I smile, because this is just too much. "No," I say, shaking my head. "And since you're clueless, you get to be Larue."

He shrugs like he could care less and points to the chair. "I do you first."

And there it is. Just as I'm turning away to sit down, I catch it. The smirk.

He is totally messing with me.

I sink into the soft leather chair and relax back against the sink. My eyes want to close immediately because this position is like a relaxation trigger. I never went to the salon much back in Chicago, but I went enough to know that Ronin is right—the shampoo comes with expectations. Elise certainly delivered the other day with me because I was willing to forget all my troubles for a few moments in her care.

Ronin gathers my hair and turns the water on. He

messes around to get the correct temperature and stays silent, which makes this whole thing on the edge of awkward. "So," I begin. "Are you a certified shampooer?"

"I'm a total professional, Rook."

"Is that right?"

"Mmmm," he says as the warm water runs over the crown of my head and tickles me.

"Most professionals would put that little bib thing on their clients, though. Right?"

"Only the ones who plan on getting their clients wet."

"So… you don't plan on getting me wet?"

He chokes down a laugh. "Be good, Gidget, or I'll have to spank you." The water stops and I smell coconuts. He rubs his hands together and lifts my wet hair from the basin, massaging the sweet-smelling soap into the longest strands first.

"I used to be blonde, ya know. In my other life."

"Huh," he says.

"What?"

"I can't see you as blonde at all. What idiot made you do that?"

"Why would someone wanting me blonde make them an idiot?" And more importantly, I ask myself, why did he suspect I was forced so quickly?

"Because you're probably the most perfect natural beauty I've ever seen, so anyone who wanted you to have blonde hair was looking to ruin you."

"Yeah, you're probably right about that."

He stops the massage on the ends of my hair. "I'm probably right? Or I am right?"

I shrug as he takes his fingertips to my scalp. His touch has just the right amount of pressure and he rubs my skin in small circles, starting from my temples and moving back down my head, and then under my neck.

My whole body erupts in chills.

"Feel good?"

"So good," I murmur, enjoying it to the fullest.

"When you do me," he says as he takes his fingertips to the top of my head, producing another wave of chills, "I like it up here."

I laugh. "Is that right? That's your big shampoo training tip, Larue? Do me like this?"

He leans all the way down into my ear, so close that my eyes shoot open when his breath tickles the sensitive skin. "Do me just like that, Rook. Please."

Oh, fuck.

I swallow, trying to stall for a response, but I have nothing. I take a chance and glance up at him. He's laughing at me. "You're bad."

"You have no idea. Now, close your eyes so I can rinse. I might make you wet, so I apologize ahead of time for that."

Oh, he is so bad.

And I am in so much trouble because even though he's very careful with the water as he rinses my head, I am definitely wet.

"So, you're a model now. Or you most likely will be tomorrow. What's your big plan? Got one?"

"Yeah," I answer, thankful that we're done with the sexual banter for now. "I'm gonna ride it out while it lasts."

"So you think you'll like being a model?"

"Maybe, but it doesn't matter. If it pays decent money I'm gonna do it." He shuts the water off and I turn a little to look up at him. "It's a break I really need, Ronin. You have no idea. So maybe I'll like doing this stuff or maybe I won't. But I'm gonna get as much out of it as I can and then, when it's over, I'll go do something else."

"Like what?" The strong smell of citrus permeates the air as he starts working in the conditioner.

My hair is so long and thick, this usually takes a while even when I'm in a rush, but Ronin takes his time and I sink into the chair a little more, totally relaxed. "College, maybe. I never got good grades, and I took the GED when I was sixteen so I could quit going to school, but I know you can start out in community college and then transfer into a better place. That's my dream. It'll probably never happen, but you asked."

"What would you study?"

"I dunno," I lie. I could just tell him, but I don't feel like it. It's my dream and it's personal. It means a lot to me and I'm not gonna share that with some guy I just met.

"What if you didn't get this job? Or what if it doesn't last? Models are known for having a pretty sketchy schedule. Work one day, none the next. It's not real stable."

This question is even worse than the last one. "Yeah, well, I'm used to disappointment, so no big deal. If it doesn't work, I'll move on and do something else. I might be young, but I've learned a few good lessons in my day."

He goes still so I open my eyes and look up at him. He's frowning. "What lessons, Rook?"

"Don't rely on anyone to get what you want. You just gotta go get it yourself."

"That's kinda sad," he says as the water comes on again.

"Nah, just practical." I shiver as the water rushes over my head.

"So you're not the type who looks for a boyfriend to take care of her?"

I snort. "Fuck. No. The last thing I want right now is

a guy who wants to take care of me."

"Huh. Well, what do you tell them then?"

"Tell who?" I ask, looking up at him again.

"The guys you date? Do you tell them you're just interested in casual stuff, or what? I don't get it."

I'm tired of this conversation so I shut it down. "I tell them nothing, Ronin, because I don't let anyone get that close."

"Because someone hurt you?" he asks, trying to sound nonchalant.

"Is this a psych couch or a shampoo station?"

He smiles down at me and shuts the water off, then wrings out my hair and drapes a towel over my head. "Sit up." He fluffs my hair with the towel for a few minutes, then tosses it into a basket across the room and hands me a comb. "So, was it everything you thought it would be?"

The innuendo is back and I smile as I drag the comb through my hair and stand up next to him. He's tricky, this one. Knows just when to light me up and dim me back down. "It was so much more," I gush, "I have no words to describe it."

"Try," he says, suddenly serious.

His hands begin to wander around my waist, tugging on my belt loops, a safe way to make contact but not put his whole hand on my hip.

I'm holding my breath and it comes out in a soft rush. "It was gentle."

He smiles.

"And it made me tingle."

"Tingle?" he asks. "Really? That good?"

I nod as I watch his lips. His mouth opens a little and I draw in a deep breath.

"Well, I'm not sure you're ready to step into my shampoo shoes, but give it a go, OK? And if you get nervous, just take a deep breath and I'll hold your hand the whole way through. From working the faucet to rinsing the conditioner, I have your back, Rook."

Never once does he crack a smile.

I nod and become very serious. "I really appreciate your confidence in me, Larue. Now, please, lie back in my chair and I'll do you just the way you like it."

Chapter Seventeen

Ronin

Rook's hands on me almost drive me over the edge. I take a deep breath as she sprays the water down my head, then leans down to talk in my ear, just the way I did with her. She's totally on to me and this makes me smile.

"What's funny, Larue?" she quips.

"You, Gidget. You think I don't know who Gidget is? *Please.*" I say it the way she did earlier, with mock exasperation. "I fangirled on Gidget *before* she was on RetroTube every night."

"You do not watch RetroTube!"

I cross my heart with my fingertips. "I swear, Gidge was my girl back when I was a boy. She's hot."

"It's the pigtails, isn't it?"

"Mmmmm, and she did this thing with her tongue…" Rook covers her mouth with her hand to hide her laugh. God, she's beautiful when she's laughing. "… and her feet. When she talked on her little pink phone her feet had this whole other conversation going on."

"Oh my God, you *are* a Gidget fan! Who would know

that?"

I open my eyes and enjoy her delight. "We have a contract coming up soon. The one you're doing is called TRAGIC, right? We have the STURGIS one and then the GIDGET one. I've been researching that little teen-flake for months now."

"So which one, Sandra Dee or Sally Field?"

"Definitely Sandy but Sally has way more episodes, so…"

"Yeah, I agree. When I was a kid I wanted to be Gidget so bad. Who's got the contract for that job?"

I look at her and it sinks in.

"Let me guess, you can't be both TRAGIC and GIDGET."

"Two totally different worlds, Rook."

She just shrugs and goes back to my hair. "How am I doing so far?"

"Magic, your fingers are magic." I close my eyes and relax again, content with how this afternoon is playing out. She's fun and easy-going. She's not offended when I flirt and she flirts back.

Water rushes down my neck and I jump out of the chair and turn back to look at her. "You got me wet!"

"Sorry, Larue. But I'm just a trainee, you can't expect me to be a professional like you on the first try."

I whip my shirt off and wipe the water off my neck. "Are you done with me?"

"I'm not sure," she replies, tilting her head coyly. "Did I do you right?"

I walk towards her and she holds her hands up and shrinks back into the corner. She's laughing so I know it's all in fun, but the defensive positioning bothers me for some reason. Like she's used to being stalked. Like she's used to guys coming at her with fists.

She starts to shift, uncomfortable with my silence and staring.

"Would you like to come upstairs with me?"

"What's upstairs?" she asks, trying to play innocent.

"My apartment. I could make you lunch." I look at the clock on the wall and it's almost dinner time, then nod towards it. "Or dunch, since it's late now."

"Dunch?"

"Yeah, you know, lunch and dinner. It's like brunch, but it's dunch."

"You cook?"

"No," I laugh. "Not really. But I can buy food and bring it back and put it on a plate and pretend I made you dunch." I walk a few paces towards her and she takes a deep breath but holds her ground. Yes, someone definitely hurt this girl in the past and that makes me angry. She catches my change in mood and I smile to ease her back down. She's perceptive.

"What else would we do?" she asks as I take her hand and pull her out of the corner.

"Watch a movie?" I offer. This piques her interest and she brightens as I bring her towards me and push her wet hair off her shoulders. It leaves drops of water behind on her bare skin.

"Which movie?" she breathes as I pull her into my chest. I can feel her heart hammering against my body and I take her face in my hands.

"Any movie you want. We have a database of pretty much everything." I lean down and caress her lips with mine and then groan when a tiny moan escapes her mouth.

She pulls back, her hand firmly against my chest to keep me at bay. "Why are you kissing me?"

"Because I can't stop myself. And because I'm the

only one who knows you, and you're just Rook, the girl who appeared out of nowhere. But tomorrow, you'll be Rook, the face of TRAGIC. And I don't think you're tragic at all, Rook. I think you're Gidget. But what I think doesn't matter, because things will move forward once you sign that contract and we'll just have to wait and see where it all ends up."

"You don't want me to sign the contract?" She scowls at me, like I'm trying to steal her future away or something.

"No, that's not it. I want you to have your chance at that dream you have, but there's a reason this campaign is called TRAGIC and not GIDGET and I'm guessing you already know that, because you look like a smart girl to me. So, just for tonight, I'd like to treat you like Gidget and have you over for dinner and a movie."

She swallows down a sad look and then paints on a smile. "OK, dinner and movie. I'd like that."

I lean down again and brush against her ear with my lips as I whisper, "But no matter what happens—you will never shrink back into a corner from me again. Because I will never hurt you."

She stiffens a little as I hold her close, but I wait for her to relax before I let her go. And then I take her hand and lead her towards the stairs.

Chapter Eighteen

Oh shit. I'm not sure what I'm doing here. Ronin is all over the place with me this weekend. Last night he had me standing in front of him naked so he could take a picture and hint that he'll take care of me. He leaves to go take care of someone else apparently, then lets himself back into my apartment and sleeps on my couch. He gives me a boat-load of free designer clothes, tests the waters with some not-so-veiled flirting, and then kisses me and invites me up to his apartment.

And I'm going!

Even though my head is screaming *stop*, my feet keep going. My hand is grasping his just as hard as he is clutching mine. My heart is pounding and if he wanted to take me to bed right now, I'd probably let him.

And on top of all that, he's got some well-formed opinions on what might have happened in my other life.

He stops at the top of the stairs and I try to rein in my wild emotions.

"Everything OK?"

I swallow and nod and this makes him frown. "What?"

"You look scared out of your freaking mind, Rook. You don't have to come up here, you know. We can go eat at Cookie's if you want."

I take a deep breath. "No, no, I want to watch a movie with you." That's not a lie either, the thought of picking a movie to watch with him actually sounds fun. "But I'm not interested in anything else." I look away, embarrassed.

"I don't want anything else, Rook. Just dinner and a movie."

I nod and snap back to reality, noting the hallway we've ended up in at the top of the stairs. Ronin notices my new interest in the place and points to the massive wooden double doors down off to the right. "That's Elise and Antoine's apartment. I'm this way." He redirects my attention to the left, where the hallway goes on for several yards and ends at an equally massive single door.

He keys in his security code and the door beeps and then clicks when the mechanism unlocks. Ronin opens the door and waves me in. I take a tentative step forward and then move out of the way so he can get past me. "Come on, I'll show you the movies."

He lets go of my hand and I scramble to take it back. He smiles over his shoulder and tugs me farther into the room. "Here's the remote," he says, motioning at me to sit on the couch. "Push that turquoise button to get to the movie database."

I push it and a search screen comes up along with a menu for different genres. "What kind of movies do you like?" I ask.

"Your pick tonight, I'll get dinner, and," he stresses, "I get to pick your food. And you can pick the movie."

"What's with you and the choosing food thing? I don't get that. Wouldn't you rather I get something I like?"

"Did you hate the burger I got you?"

"No, but—"

"But nothing. Give me a chance. I promise, I'm good at this."

"Yeah, but it's weird."

"What's weird about ordering you food?"

"It's not the ordering, it's the control."

"Oh, I get it. You're one of those."

"Those what?"

"Control freaks. You have to be in control all the time, right?"

"What? That's so far from the truth it's bizarre."

"What else could be then? I mean, if I pick what you like, then why do you care if I order you food?"

And I'm trapped. I can only shrug because to tell him the truth will spill all my secrets and to deny it will just keep the conversation going. Luckily he's one of those graceful winners and shoots me a wink.

"I'll be back in like twenty, OK?"

I nod and relax back into the overstuffed couch as Ronin walks down the hallway and comes back with a clean shirt, then heads out. My gaze wanders around the room and I take it all in. It's definitely a guy's apartment because the color scheme is nothing but shades of brown with some black thrown in for variety. He has the biggest TV screen I've ever seen hanging on the wall and I get a little chill of delight as I think about watching movies on that thing. He's got surround sound speakers placed strategically around the room and through the sheer curtains I can see the city lights across what seems to be a pretty significant terrace.

Man, these people definitely have money.

I take my attention back to the database and enter the movie I want to watch. I've been thinking about this movie since I met him actually, because of his name. It's a movie both of us can enjoy—a touching love story with beautiful scenery—cherry blossoms even. And it's a war movie with lots of blood and gore.

I think he'll love it. This makes me warm because if I'm honest, I want him to love it. Because I love it.

I really don't have a lot of experience with men but I can say with absolute certainty that no man has ever looked at me the way Ronin Flynn did when I came out of that closet wearing the blue nightie. His eyes swept down my body in hungry desire and then they climbed back up so slowly my heart started pounding with the anticipation of what his expression would say when he finally found my face.

If I spoke the language of his eyes I'd know for certain, but I'm at a loss with this guy. I'm fumbling around in the dark trying not to look or act like a complete child and I hope I'm not wrong about my guess, but those eyes looked like they wanted to touch every part of my body.

In the few seconds we twined our gaze together I heard myself ask him to kiss me a million ways in my thoughts, and if I spoke the language of my own desire then I'd know for certain that I almost begged him to do it with the look on my face.

Touch me, I should've whispered. *Kiss me*. Because my whole body is humming with the realization that this is how a man makes you feel when you actually like him. This is what girls mean when they claim a man makes them feel weak. They don't picture fists hovering over them as they cower in the corner, hoping and praying that those hands never connect with their cheekbone.

I press play on the screen and then pause the movie and go over to the terrace to wait for Ronin. It's not warm out, but it's tolerable for a spring evening so I slip out and leave the door open behind me. It's a pretty large square terrace filled with patio furniture and a grill off to the side.

I walk over to the railing, bend down a little, and rest my chin on my hands. The view of downtown Denver is stunning—the tall buildings are lit up and everything seems to twinkle. I have no idea what any of the buildings are, but I don't care either. They're pretty. It's amazing, when I think about it, how fast things can change. Three months ago I was an abused girlfriend, beaten to within an inch of her life. Three days ago I was a scared girl with very little money in a strange city and living in a homeless shelter.

And tonight, even though I'm still scared and I still have very little money, it's all flipped around. I'm in a fantastic apartment with a beautiful man. I'm wearing some pretty nice clothes that I'll probably regret asking for when I see how much they cost. And I might even have a job as a model for a photographer who is important enough to own an entire building and pay girls a hundred dollars an hour to sit for him.

I hear the soft footsteps but I don't turn.

"Find a movie you like?" he asks as he comes up behind me. He puts his hands on either side of the railing, my body between them, and then takes a chance and leans in to close the distance between us.

"Yes," I reply as his mouth dips down to my neck, sending a tingle all the way up my body.

"What're you thinking about, if you don't mind me asking?"

I sigh. "Just how funny life can be. How things can change in a moment and how you never know when that moment will come. It's occurred to me over the past few days that I'm not really in control of very much. I mean, I can make a decision to get on a bus and move to a new city completely alone. And I can make the decision to walk out of a job where I was being falsely accused of stealing. And I can make the decision to spend my last ten dollars on a coffee where a bunch of models fling a little white card at my face and I end up with an invitation to sit in front of Antoine Chaput."

I turn my body so I'm facing him. I wonder what he thinks of that little revelation? That I wasn't invited, but stole an opportunity to test for Antoine from another girl. He eases up to let me turn, but as soon as I'm settled he presses against me again, only this time his chest is touching my breasts instead of my back, and his hands slip under my hair and begin to caress my neck. If he has an opinion on the invitation, he holds it back.

"But everything after that was luck," I continue. "I can't control other people. I couldn't make Elise take me into the studio, or Antoine like the way I look, or get offered a fake job shampooing hair just so I'd stick around."

He grins at that last remark.

"And I have no control over how you feel about me or why you want to let me stay here." I stare into his eyes and shrug. "I'm totally at the mercy of the universe for these parts. And it's a little bit scary not to be in control, don't you think?"

He pulls my face closer to his and my heart pounds with the thought of another kiss. But he doesn't kiss me, at least not where I expect him to. He brings his lips to my forehead and crushes himself to me, breathing in deeply. And his hands play with my hair, still stringy and damp from my shampoo.

"It's very scary," he whispers as his mouth travels down to my ear. "And I don't know the whole story with you but if you really did all that then I'm in awe of your courage, Rook."

"I think you overestimate me, Ronin. It wasn't courage, it was desperation and fear."

He pulls me all the way into him then, pressing me up against his chest, his hands wrapped tightly around my head and neck in a protective embrace. "Even so. You came up with a plan, and that is courage. Because if this guy you're running from did the things I think he did, then I know first-hand how scary that is."

I push back and stare up at him. "How?" I ask.

He smiles but it's sad. "Because my father used to beat the shit out of my mom back when Elise and I were kids. And one day he hit her with a baseball bat and she never got back up. Elise was eighteen and I was ten when they took my dad to prison. He's still there, I think. I have no idea really. When Antoine showed up and wanted to date Elise and take me in, we stopped being those tragic kids and just went back to being us again. It was scary as fuck those first few years, having to trust that Antoine was good and that he'd stick around. He and Elise never married and this bothered me for a very long time. I always felt that my new life was a rug that was about to be pulled out from under me at any moment. But then, slowly, things started to change. Antoine is a good guy, he loves Elise, and yeah, I'd like him to marry her and give her more security—but if what they have is good enough for Elise, then I just have to accept it."

It's my turn to wrap my hands around his neck and pull him close. I can't reach his forehead so I kiss his chin instead and he laughs. "Sorry," I say with a smile. "I can't reach your forehead but I wanted to kiss you."

He leans down and takes my lips this time, a soft, slow kiss that makes my toes feel warm. The heat climbs up my body as his mouth opens a little and I'm throbbing between my legs in seconds.

I pull back.

"Ronin Flynn, you might undo me."

"I'm already undone, Gidge. I'm just hoping you'll stick around long enough to put me back together."

Chapter Nineteen

Ronin

We go back inside and get our food. I got her another burger. Since I flapped my mouth about picking something she likes, and I know she likes burgers and salads with chicken on them, I got the burger again. She laughs and calls me a cheat, but eats every bite and this makes me so happy I can't stand it.

Even though my general rule is no models in the bedroom, I've dated them before and I know each and every one of them has an eating disorder. Maybe it never gets serious, maybe it only manifests as small, barely noticeable rationing, but we all know that if the girls get too big, they can't wear the clothes. And if they can't wear the clothes, they're out of a job.

Rook doesn't know this yet, but it won't take her long to figure it out. And I like her the way she is—her body is fucking hot. And I think it might break my heart if she traded those curves in for bones.

"So what movie are we watching?" I ask.

"*The Last Samurai*," she says with a coy grin.

"You think you're clever, don't you, Gidget? Got it all figured out?" She plops down on the couch and I sit just far enough away to make her wonder what my intentions are. I have no intentions. Well, maybe I do, but they are fairly innocent right now.

"I have no idea what you're talking about. This movie has Tom I-have-no-shirt-on-and-I-kill-people-with-swords Cruise in it."

She's got me here. "So you have no idea what my name means?"

"Hmmm," she says. "Larue, that's French, right?"

I laugh. "Really? You have no idea?"

She smiles and leans back into the couch, her cute little bare feet doing a dance as they rest on the coffee table. "Everything I do is done with purpose, Ronin. The waitress wrote your name on the ticket that first night I ate at Cookie's, so I knew right then it wasn't Irish, even though your last name is Flynn and that *is* Irish. But I didn't choose this movie to impress you with my knowledge of your name."

I laugh again. Like hell she didn't.

"I chose it because it's got cherry trees, is deeply philosophical, and is cinematically beautiful."

I just stare at her.

"And because Tom Cruise gets to kick ass with a stick."

"Bokken," I correct her as I smile with satisfaction. I kick my feet up on the coffee table next to hers and click play on the remote. Every time she opens her mouth she surprises me. "So tomorrow, you have any questions about tomorrow?"

"Just wash the heads, right? And do them like I did you?"

My grin is so big now I have to hide it with my hand

as I look over at her. "You're bad."

"No," she says as she lies down and rests her head on my thigh. "I'm good, I swear. I'm Gidget, remember? Not tragic."

I play with her hair and watch the movie and before I know it, we're curled up together on the couch, her back pressing against my chest and my arm tucked around her middle, breathing deeply and falling asleep.

Chapter Twenty

I've always been a deep sleeper but how Ronin got his hand under my shirt and cupping my breast is a little beyond the scope of any past sleeping experiences I've ever had with an almost complete stranger. I'm not sure what to do. Besides his hold on one of my girls, he's got his other hand very low down on my belly. Pretty much slipped inside the waistband of my jeans, it's dangerously close to descending past a point of no return.

And I'm basically lying here with a racing heart from these simple touches. I cannot even imagine how turned on I'd be if his fingers slid between my legs.

I'd be undone for sure.

He's also pressing himself up against my ass, making it hard to ignore a feature of men in the morning the world over. The wood.

I giggle a little at my thoughts and he stirs awake.

Oh, shit! Now he's gonna wonder why I didn't move his hands!

I'm saved by a loud knock on the door.

"Shit," Ronin says, obviously awake because that was not a husky I-just-woke-up voice. He disentangles himself from me and makes his way to the door.

It's Elise. I can sorta hear them, but not really because they talk low. I do catch something about me being here and then it sounds like Elise is asking a bunch of questions. I sit up on the couch and straighten out my shirt, feeling a little bit like an intruder as I wait for the conversation to be over.

The door closes with a quiet little click and then Ronin comes around the corner and smiles. "Sorry, didn't mean to wake you."

"What time is it? I can't believe I slept here on your couch."

"It's five thirty, and I enjoyed you sleeping here. I hope you'll do it again tonight, actually."

"Oh," is all I can say to that.

He shoots me a grin. "But right now I'm gonna walk you back to the garden apartment so you can sleep in. Mondays are crazy busy and Elise just excused you from shampoo duty. She says for you to come by the salon around two o'clock. That sound cool?"

I make a face. "So I have to spend the whole day in my apartment?"

He shrugs. "You can spend it here if you want, but it's gonna get noisy."

"No, I didn't mean that, I just meant..." What the hell did I mean? "Never mind, yeah, it's better to go back to my apartment. I need to hang up all those clothes anyway. What should I wear when I show up for Elise?"

"Jeans, whatever. She'll tell you what she wants you to wear."

"Oh," I say again. "I thought you ran the clothes?"

"I do, but I have to take care of something today.

That's what Elise came to tell me. So I'll miss your big debut and we'll do those cherry tree pics tomorrow."

I shrug on the outside, but inside I'm wondering just what this is all about. He's got to leave for an entire day? I slip my Converse on and he opens the front door for me. I feel a little cheap as I make my way down the stairs and then when he says goodbye at the terrace door, holding it open for me so I can pass through alone, I almost feel dirty.

I'm not even sure where this feeling is coming from, I mean I didn't sleep with him or anything. I just feel like he's trying to get rid of me before anyone figures out I spent the night at his house.

I turn to say goodbye, but the door is already swinging closed. So I pad over to my own place, let myself in, and flop down on the couch, trying very hard not to feel used.

But Rook, the internal monologue starts, *you know he's a player. He's a male model for Pete's sake. His job is 'running the girls' at a major photography studio.*

Maybe I should take the money I make today and leave?

I can get on the bus and go to Vegas like I planned. Denver was never my original stop anyway. I was on the bus to Vegas but—well, it's a long story but I never intended to stay here in Denver. I mean who lives in Denver anyway? Not that it will be any better in Vegas, but I feel like my life is out of control right now. Like I'm not in charge of myself. And the last time I felt this way it was because my ex was the one controlling me.

I don't want to be controlled so if I made the decision to leave, then I could take that control back. If I stay here, then Ronin and Antoine and Elise have control over me, no matter how subtle.

Ughhh. Why can't life be simple?

I start picking through my new clothes, hanging up the ones that need hanging and folding the ones that need to get put away in drawers. It occurs to me pretty quickly that I have one pair of shoes and that's it. My Converse will not cut it if I want to go somewhere in a skirt.

After I hang stuff I tackle the dresser drawers. I open up the top drawer to put the underwear away and get a surprise.

This drawer is full.

Of underwear.

What the fuck?

I mean, I realize Elise said another girl used to live here, but she left her underwear? And that explains the make-up in the bathroom. And all the shampoo and soaps and stuff. Yeah, another girl lived here, but she left so fast she didn't even bother to take her very expensive-looking undergarments?

Wait a minute. These underwear are all brand new, they have tags on them.

I sit down on the bed and shake my head. What the hell can that mean? They stock this place with new underwear and makeup for... what? What reason could they have?

Maybe they have so many girls come through here I'm just another temporary occupant?

I am so confused. I mean, when Ronin is around everything feels right about this place. I feel comfortable around him, he makes me laugh, I make him laugh. We have what appears to be an easy friendship.

But every time I get away from him, all these things that might seem cozy and comfortable start to make me claustrophobic and paranoid. And I'm not really in a good place right now to be able to distinguish between the two.

I can't really trust myself to see the difference between what is normal and what isn't because I've lived with abnormal for too long.

The only thing I really do know is that I need this job. No matter what's going on here, I need this job. And then once I get some money I'll bail and head west like I planned and forget all about Ronin the rogue samurai and the whole Antoine Chaput debacle. Maybe I'll go to LA, that's where people who want to go to film school live, right? I'll find a cheap apartment, get a roommate, live there for the required year to get in-state tuition, and then get my ass into some community college and finally get my life on track.

Ronin Flynn might be hot, he might have manners, and he might have a soft side—but he's definitely not settle-down material and he certainly seems to have a problem with letting a woman make her own decisions. And I'm not ready to hand that back over again.

I'd rather spend the rest of my life alone and lonely than give up my freedom again. I need to keep my eye on the prize. And that means no more flirting with Ronin, no matter what.

Chapter Twenty-One

I lie in my new comfortable bed for a while and then let myself doze for a few hours before I have to go meet Elise. When I get up I take a bath but don't wash my hair because I figure I'll get the whole hair treatment in the salon. Plus, the same claw-foot tub that looked vintage and charming when I first saw it now looks old and dingy.

It's not charming, it's a major pain in the ass.

When I'm clean and dressed I head out to the terrace and steady myself for the day.

It's only one, so I have an hour before Elise needs me, but I figure I can get acclimated to whatever it is that's going on in the studio. I pull the doors open and I'm immediately assaulted with the bustle of people. There is laughing, talking, cameras going crazy, lights being moved, a few squeals from the girls, frantic rushing into and out of the dressing room and pretty much every degree of chaos you can think of crammed into this one room.

There are several photographers and that surprises

me. I expected that Antoine was the only one who worked here because of how quiet it was last week. But today there are no fewer than four people taking pictures as I stand there.

There are also girls, in various stages of dress, everywhere. Two are naked. Granted, the naked ones are all in the middle of a session with their respective photographers, but still.

Naked.

I am not doing *anything* naked.

A few of the girls look over at me and point, then whisper to each other. I look around, then down. Not sure what to do.

"Rook!" Elise's voice bellows out of the cacophony of noise. "I'm ready, sweetie, come in here!" She disappears behind the salon wall and I follow her.

"Did you sleep well?" Elise asks as she takes me by the arm and leads me over to the shampoo station, then pushes me into the chair.

That question sounds loaded, but I choose to ignore that and answer honestly. "Yes, great, thanks."

If she's interested in that answer she doesn't show it because the water is streaming down my head and she's busy doing her job. It's not relaxing like it was last time, it's tense. My whole neck is tense, even as she does a little scalp massage.

"Ronin won't be back until tonight. He asked me to tell you."

"OK, thanks," I manage to say as she rinses and then applies some conditioner to my long tresses.

"I'm going to have Josie trim your hair. You need it badly."

"OK." I agree because what am I gonna say? I figure that was not really a question, just a statement of facts.

Rook, I control you now, so I'm going to have someone cut your hair.

"Then you'll sit for Roger. Antoine has to do some retakes, so he can't shoot you today. Roger is good, though. That's one thing you can count on here—everyone does their job well or they are asked to leave."

This sounds like a warning, but maybe I should be thankful? It gives me some control back. If I do my job well I can stay. If I don't, then I can go. It's up to me really. I'm not exactly sure what's all entailed in doing a good job at modeling, but I imagine it has a lot to do with following directions.

And that rubs me wrong too. Because that takes away the control I'm trying to talk myself into thinking I have.

Who am I kidding? I'm not in control at all.

Elise is done with my hair so she pushes on me to sit up. The water drips all over my t-shirt and she rubs the towel over my head, but my hair is so long it spills out and drags the water along with it.

"I like your shirt. I have one like that too, we did a shoot for them a few months ago."

I look up at her to see if she's joking, but she's not paying attention to me, she's calling for Josie to come do my trim. "It came from your closet, Ronin said I could have it," I confess.

She looks back at me and smiles. "Oh good. We have hundreds of them left. I like it but shit, ya know? A hundred of them is too many. All the girls took what they wanted, you take as many as you like."

She introduces Josie and I don't even bother contradicting the fact that Elise just told her to remove four freaking inches off the length of my hair. I just sit still and let them control me because all I can think about is how Ronin picked this shirt for me, so maybe he knew they had so many no one would care? I thought it was nice until I learned it was unwanted.

I snort out a laugh at the absurdity of my reasoning.

"You OK, sweetie?"

What's with the sweetie stuff around here? Is this how grown women talk to each other? "Yeah," I mumble. "Just thinking of something." I sit quietly after that and just let Josie do her thing. When she's done cutting she starts blow-drying, Elise is busy with another girl on the other side of the salon, but when she's done she comes back and begins to wrap my hair in hot rollers. "Roger wants big bouncy curls, he said. So, that's what you get today."

"OK." That's pretty much the extent of my vocabulary right now. *Just agree, Rook. Just agree and take your money and then you'll have more choices, but right now, you just have to do what you're told.*

When she's done Elise ushers me over to another part of the salon and someone applies makeup while another girl does my nails. "You need toes today, honey?"

I shrug. That's not a question I can answer with OK. The would-be pedicurist leaves to ask Elise, and I can hear Elise become frustrated and tell her to get busy on my feet.

I've never had a pedicure, and maybe if I was paying for it and I was somewhere I could relax, I might enjoy it. But right now the last thing I want is this woman touching my toes. I balk a little when she starts rubbing cream on them, but she mistakes that for being ticklish. "Don't worry, hun. I'm not a tickler. You'll be fine."

I suck in a deep breath and let them do their thing.

When I'm done my hair is filled with loose bouncy curls, my nails and toes are both cherry red, and my make-up has me looking like I should be walking Colfax with the whores.

Elise comes back as I sit there, feeling stupid and fake. The other girls are on a break and the place has quieted down considerably since my arrival. For some reason I imagined models and artsy photographers as being afternoon people, but what do I know?

"OK, Rook. You're up." She thrusts a garment bag at me. "Since you've met the dressing room, go on and get dressed—only put on what's in the bag. When you're done, go find Roger, he's the blond one."

I don't even get to say OK this time. She walks off, calling for someone else.

Chapter Twenty Two

The dressing room has a few girls in it, but they ignore me and concentrate on themselves.

I take the hint and do the same.

Or I try to, because they are all naked and I'm just not ready to get naked in the middle of the room with these girls.

A tiny girl, someone who looks like the opposite of the image you have in your head when you say the word model, stops in front of me and smiles. "First day?"

I try not to notice she's got no shirt on, but I think I fail. "Yeah."

She nods her head towards the other side of the room. "There's privacy stalls over there if you need one." And then she saunters off, her long blonde hair bouncing along her butt.

Modest these girls are not. I look down at myself and get a sick feeling. I'm not sure I can get naked in front of them so I opt for the private dressing rooms.

The outfit was not what I was expecting. In fact, I

almost laugh when I take it out of the garment bag. It's a pair of well-worn jeans and a dark red t-shirt. Both of which look like they came from the men's department so they are monumentally too big for me, but I do what I was told, pull on the jeans, and slip the shirt over my head. There's no bra or panties in the bag, so I'm commando on both ends.

When I study myself in the mirror I can only sigh. Why did Elise get me all made up just to wear some old, half-ripped jeans and a cruddy t-shirt?

I walk out barefoot, because there were no shoes in the bag either.

At first I figured finding Roger could not be that hard, but there are no blond guys with cameras, so I just stand there until one of the girls comes out of the dressing room and I grab her attention real quick. "Roger?" I ask, as if that explains everything. She points to a guy who is sitting on a table on the far side of the studio. I turn to say thank you, but the girl is gone.

I take a deep breath and walk over towards Roger. He spies me coming from a distance and walks to meet me.

Well, that was nice.

"Ruth?"

"Ah, no. I'm Rook."

"Rook, right. That's what I meant. OK, Antoine just wants the standard portrait shots and then if we have time, I'll take some artistic ones of you and Billy since he has the other half of this outfit on."

He points to a shaggy-haired guy across the room who is also wearing an old pair of weathered jeans and a red t-shirt. Only his are much smaller than mine. "Maybe they got the clothes mixed up?" I say out loud before I can stop myself.

Roger laughs. "Why do you say that?"

"Well, his clothes look awfully tight and mine are awfully loose. It makes no sense."

He eyes me cautiously. "You're really new, aren't you?"

"First day," I reply as the nervousness appears in my stomach as a billion butterflies. "Why? Is there some secret about the clothing sizes that I should know about?"

He shrugs. "Ready then? Go stand over there and then we'll adjust the lights." I do as I'm told and stand on a little x taped to the floor. He's got four helpers just for us and they bustle around with lighting things and the background image, which is just black.

And that's pretty much where my thoughts stop. The rest is just turning and looking, and changing position, and closing my eyes, then opening them. I do a whole lot of things—standing, sitting, kneeling.

But the one thing I never get asked to do is smile.

Again.

This is weird to the point of almost being creepy because the last time I was here Antoine never asked me to smile either.

"OK, Rook, go grab Billy over there and we'll set up for the artistic shots."

I nod out a yes, but this makes me jitter with nervousness. I walk slowly over towards the Billy guy. His shoot is over and he's just hanging out with a girl.

A girl who looks pretty pissed off that I just walked up to them and interrupted.

"Uh, sorry. Excuse me, Billy? Roger asked me to come get you."

The girl sneers at me then kisses Billy, drags her fingernail down his chest, and whispers, "Call me later," as she saunters off. I watch her for several seconds before turning back.

Billy is watching me.

I smile.

He sighs and walks over towards Roger.

Shit, these people are not as friendly as I'd hoped. Even Elise was kinda short and testy with me today. I look up at a giant clock on the wall and wonder when the day will end. It's already almost six o'clock and I'm very hungry. I munched on my take-home breakfast from Cookie's the other day, but that was right after I came home from Ronin's and I didn't have any lunch. Maybe this is why models are so skinny—there's no food around!

I reach Roger a few seconds after Billy and they are already positioning him on a bed that has somehow materialized. My heart beats a little faster and my eyes dart around to try and figure out what we're doing.

"Relax, Rook. There's a reason for the loose clothing, it's so that when Billy here gropes you the clothes show some skin. So go ahead and sit down next to him and we'll get this started."

Gropes me? I'm thinking I'm saying that out loud, but I'm not. So no one explains, but Billy does get up and take my hand and leads me over to the bed.

"First time?" he asks casually as we stand there.

"What?"

"For an artistic shoot? I haven't seen you around before and you look pretty nervous."

"I am," I confess. "I've never done this before."

He slips his hand up my shirt and all I hear is the rapid clicking of a camera shutter. I look around and the shoot has started.

"Don't worry, it'll be quick." He tugs on my shirt, exposing my belly, then pulls it up and leans in to kiss me. I don't know what I'm thinking but I let him. This is work, right? This is what they do? Kiss each other?

I have no idea, but his hands are all over me, his mouth is traveling down my neck fast, and I'm starting to shake.

"Easy," he whispers. "He won't shoot long. Just listen to me, OK?"

I nod.

"Just let me do my thing, pretend you're in love with me and my hands are a gift from God, and he'll get his shots and we can go eat or something."

Is he asking me out? I am so confused but I do what I'm told. It's not that hard, Billy is doing all the work, really. His hands do the groping, pulling the red shirt this way and that, exposing my skin, my belly here, parts of my breast there. It's OK. This is work.

"OK, Rook," Roger says, interrupting my thoughts. "Take his shirt off, *slowly*."

Oh, shit.

"Any day now, Rook."

I nod. OK. I lift up the bottom of his shirt—

"Slower, Rook."

Right. Slowly.

"Now look at him while you do it."

This gets very personal, very fast. Because Billy here has a hard-on, I can feel it as he presses his leg against my hip, and his eyes look like he's about to throw me down on the bed and make me scream his name right here in front of the whole studio filled with people.

"Keep working, Rook."

I tug the shirt up again and Billy lets out a moan. "Shit, Rook," he says. "You're sexy. I don't even have to try."

I do try… and ignore him, that is. But it's pretty hard when Roger is constantly telling me to look Billy in the eyes. Finally, *finally* I get the shirt over his head and then he starts on mine.

"Am I supposed to take my shirt off?"

"Just go with it, Rook, or we'll be here all fucking night."

Billy leans in to kiss me and the shutter goes wild again.

"Slower this time, Billy. I need lips for stock art."

Billy slows down and takes his time coming at me.

"Rook, either respond or we'll have to do it again."

I do my best, but I'm not that great of a kisser and Billy here is doing enough for both of us. His hands slip around my waist, pulling me close. "Touch me, Rook, let the man get his photos."

I allow my hands to travel up his torso and feel a shiver burst from his skin. My body responds the same way as his hand slips under my shirt and then he spins me around, lifting the loose fabric up as his hand explores my breast. He's kissing my neck and tugging on the jeans. They are so loose, they almost fall down my hips. This makes Roger call out a "Nice, Billy! Do that some more," to which Billy responds by slipping his hand right between my legs.

I let out a giant gasp and Billy is about to swipe my shirt clean off when Ronin is up in his face screaming. "What the fuck are you doing?"

I'm discarded by Billy, instantly forgotten as the two of them push each other.

Roger is trying to run interference and then Ronin pushes Billy so hard he comes hurtling towards me, knocking against my shoulder, and sends me crashing to the ground.

Everything stops.

Everyone looks.

And then Elise is pulling me up and shoving me

towards the stairs as Antoine and several other people pull Billy and Ronin apart.

"I fucking told you portraits, Antoine! What the fuck is going on here?"

"Go upstairs and wait for Ronin, Rook," Elise says sternly, like this is somehow my fault.

I start walking, watching them fight.

What just happened?

I get to Ronin's apartment but the door is locked, so I go back and sit on the top step because I can't even remember my birthday right now, let alone his security code. I just sit there and listen to them all argue inside Antoine's office. The door is closed, I can tell by the muffled voices, but it's not sound-proof.

The yelling gets louder and then the door opens because the voices are like right there, echoing off the massive walls of the studio. Almost everyone has cleared out now, and then I watch Ronin as he takes the stairs three at a time. When he gets to me he stops.

Just stops. There are no hurried words or fast actions. He is just still.

"I'm sorry, I told Antoine what I wanted, but he forgot to tell Roger. It was a mistake. I'm sorry."

"What was a mistake?"

"That shoot with fucking Billy!"

He says it like he can't believe I had to ask, so I just nod. "Right, OK."

He takes my hand and leads me towards his apartment, then he must spy my bare feet. "Where're your shoes?"

"The dressing room, with my clothes."

"OK," he says, pushing me through the apartment door, "I'll get them, you stay here."

I stand in the middle of the room, watching the

empty space where he just was.

This whole thing is getting weird. I might need to go back to the shelter. This thought makes me swallow down a giant lump in my throat because I really do not want to go back there.

Ronin takes forever, so I just take a seat on the couch and wait. Still, he does not come back. I lie down and close my eyes. I have to admit, even after all I've been through in the past few months, this has been one of the longest and most confusing days of my entire life.

Chapter Twenty-Three

Rook

I wake abruptly as Ronin adjusts my body so my head is resting in his lap. "What?"

"Sorry," he says. "You fell asleep and I just wanted to sit with you. Rook, I am so sorry about earlier. Antoine said he was going to do the shoot himself, I asked him to keep an eye on you. It shouldn't have happened."

I sit up, the make-up from earlier making my face feel caked with filth, and I'm almost positive that it's totally streaked all over my face. I have like a ton of goop in my eyes and it's taking every ounce of self-control not to rub them red. "What *was* supposed to happen?"

"Just some portrait pics, that's all. I told him."

"Well, that Roger guy did take a bunch of those. I know that for sure. Then he said I was dressed for an artistic shoot with Billy and—"

"Yeah, fucking Roger knows better. We don't stick new girls with Billy."

I take a deep breath and turn to look at him. "Ronin, why don't you tell me exactly what you guys do here? Is it porn, or what?"

"No," he says quickly. "It's not porn, it's… erotic art."

"Uh-huh. Erotic art. So what exactly do you guys want me for? Just so we're clear."

"Pictures."

"Of me naked?"

"No… I mean… well, somewhat naked, yes. We're not doing cock shots or shit like that, Rook. It's tasteful nudes and stuff."

I laugh as I stand up. "OK, I'm probably gonna have to leave. I mean, I'm not against doing some pictures, even some racy ones, but I need to think about it and see how much money it pays and I'm not comfortable doing that here. So I'm gonna go back to the shelter for a while and you guys call me if—"

"Absolutely not, Rook! You're not going to a fucking homeless shelter. We're having dinner with Antoine and Elise in an hour to sort it all out, you can't leave before you at least get all the details."

I hesitate because I don't want to go back to the shelter, I mean, I would almost rather sleep anywhere else but there, so I hesitate.

"Just go take a shower, put on your own clothes, and let's have dinner, OK?"

I am seriously starving and my rumbling stomach wins the night. I can at least hear them out. "OK." He sighs with relief. "I would like to take a shower, actually."

His eyes light up. "That's the best news I've heard all day. Follow me, I'll introduce you to the beast."

I follow him into the bathroom off the hallway and he's not kidding. The shower is a beast. It's a massive work of tiled art with more knobs and shower heads than I can even imagine are necessary.

He sees me eyeing them suspiciously. "Don't even

ask, Rook. I have no idea what they all do. But if you press this button here"—he points to something that looks like a security system control panel—"then they all come on at once and I'll just warn you now, that shit is better than sex."

"Oh," I moan, "that's too bad. I totally thought the only way I'd feel better tonight was if I could just get me some sex, but now that I have this here shower, I guess I'm good."

"You're OK, then?" He takes my joking as a good sign, but honestly, it's my default setting. When I get nervous and I'm not in danger of getting my face punched in, I tend to turn into a smart-ass.

"I'm really not, but I'm trying real hard, Ronin."

He walks over to me, doesn't touch me, but gets close enough so that we don't need to touch to understand what's going on. I can feel his presence, like his body has an electric field around it and I've suddenly found myself inside. I have to look up at him because now that we're standing right up next to each other I realize how tall he is. At least five inches taller than me and I'm five nine.

"Just give us a chance, OK? If you don't want the job I'll understand. But this day should not have happened this way."

He watches me intently but I'm not capable of talking about this right now. I need some space. "Can you go get me some clothes from the apartment? I'll even let you pick them."

"Yeah, sure. I'll just turn on the shower for you." He messes with the control panel and water starts spraying out in all directions. I smile a thank you and he leaves, closing the door behind him.

When I looking the bathroom mirror I was right about the make-up—it is totally smeared under my eyes.

The beastly shower feels better than ever right now. My body is tired and not eating right is not helping. I hope they are having something good for dinner because if it's some French shit, I might scream and throw a fit until they feed me a burger or take me to the baseball stadium for a hot dog.

When I'm done I wrap the towel around me and open the door cautiously, I can hear Ronin talking on the phone. I listen for a few seconds, but it's all in French and I only catch the name Clare. There's a small pile of clothes on the floor in front of the bathroom and I grab them and disappear back inside. He picked me out a very sweet white bra and panty set, some pink capris, a pink tank top, and a white cotton button-up sweater. I slip on my beat-up old Converse because they're all I have. When I look in the mirror my long black hair contrasts with the cute outfit and I suddenly feel like biker Gidget.

He was so right last night—I'm no Gidget. I'm definitely a tragic if ever there was one.

Ronin is sitting on his couch watching sports when I come back out.

"Feel better?"

I nod. "Yeah, I do."

He gets up, takes my hand, and then we walk down the hallway towards the stairs. It's so quiet compared to earlier I almost don't recognize the studio as we walk past and continue down the hall. Ronin punches in a code, opens the door and waves me in first.

Antoine and Elise are nowhere to be found, so I take a moment to study the apartment. It's like stepping back into the Roaring Twenties. The whole inside looks like something off *The Great Gatsby* movie set, it's all curves and contrasts—art deco from top to bottom. The furniture is ultra-modern but old and stylish at the same time. The chairs and couches have high curved backs, and the black piping on the cushions perfectly sets off the white fabric.

The far side of the room is one giant circular window that has pocket glass doors to allow access to the terrace. This is where the voices are coming from and Ronin leads me through the portal-like door. Exiting onto the terrace is like stepping into another world. There are twinkling white lights strung everywhere and the terrace itself is massive. Like bigger than the first floor of the house I lived in back in Chicago. It's furnished like the inside, except with weatherproof fabrics.

Ronin calls out a, "Hey." And both Antoine and Elise pull apart from an embrace like two school kids caught necking in the hallways.

Did I just use the word necking?

The Gidget outfit is getting to me, I think.

"I hope you like kebabs," Ronin says. "Antoine makes some of the best kebabs ever."

"If it's meat, I'll eat it," I reply, my stomach growling like mad with the smell that wafts off the grill and teases my senses.

"You wanna beer?"

"Sure." This is already turning out to be way better than I imagined, so why not relax a little. In my head dinner with the Chaputs involved a white tablecloth, crystal glassware, and eating snails drowning in butter with tiny little forks.

Ronin grabs a Corona from a box filled with ice and twists off the cap, then hands it to me and takes one for himself. He grabs two lime wedges from a little silver bucket in the ice, and shoves down the neck of each beer. I enjoy the smell of a fizzy lime-infused beer and then take a long gulp.

Elise walks over to us. "How old are you, Rook?"

"Twenty-one."

"Really?"

"Shut up, Elise, like you waited until you were twenty-one to drink. Leave her alone, she's here to relax."

Elise narrows her eyes at Ronin and then looks over to me. "I wasn't asking because of the beer, I just need to know for our contracts. Are you really twenty-one?"

"No, I'm nineteen," I say, a little ashamed as I try and hand the beer back to Ronin. He shakes his head at me and I keep the beer.

"I'm not interested in policing your alcohol habits, Rook. This is a working dinner, sweetie, and it involves contracts so I just want to make sure you are legal to sign them. We need to get some things straight and we need to know what you will and won't be doing for us while you're working here."

I swallow. Boy, she really gets to the point.

"Because while we feel what we do here is art, not everyone agrees and you need to know what it means for you to agree to model for us. OK?"

I nod.

"So Ronin, why don't you go keep Antoine company while Rook and I go over the particulars."

"You OK with this, Rook?" he asks.

"Yeah, sure. It's business."

He smiles and walks over to Antoine, who has switched the conversation to French. I can hear Ronin say, "English, you ape," as he approaches.

"Have a seat, Rook." I look back to Elise, who is all business right now. Gone is that little fairy woman who took pity on me as I cried on the stairs and I'm sorta sorry she got to see me in such a weak position, it puts me behind right now. Like she knows I'm not strong so she automatically gets the upper hand.

I sit like I'm told and wait for it.

"OK, I'm not going to sugarcoat it because I'm hungry and I try and treat everyone the same, and I don't sugarcoat it for any of the other models, so you are no different just because Ronin wants to keep you."

"What?"

"He likes you, Rook, I think we can both agree that is true. So what I want you to know up front is that we are an erotic photography studio, we supply photos, *tasteful photos*," she enunciates, "to companies like publishers, producers, large marketing firms and the like. They typically come in an order that asks for something specific, but if we have images we can't use, leftovers and such, we sell them to stock art companies. Do you know what that is, Rook? Stock art?"

I shake my head.

"It's a database of photos on a large website that allows anyone to buy the images for a fee and use them as they see fit for projects, with certain restrictions regarding print production. So this means, should you sign our model release form, your body could end up pretty much anywhere. On the cover of a book, in an advertisement, a CD cover, things like that. Do you understand this?"

"Yes, I understand."

"Good. So here's the deal. You don't have to do nudes. We have some work for you that is straight portrait and fashion, a bit of glamour stuff every now and then like Clare does. You'll make twenty dollars an hour and that's it. You work by the hour and the work for these types of shots is not steady, but since Ronin seems compelled to take care of you, you hardly need the money."

I'm not sure why, but I take offense to this statement.

"Ronin would prefer this option, but you should know that if you get a private contract—for instance, if you agree to do the TRAGIC campaign we are setting up—you will make thousands of dollars. Many thousands of dollars. This contract has a budget of two hundred and fifty thousand dollars and a portion of that is for the models. If you're chosen and you agree, you'll make a lot of money. This is what we do here. We make a lot of money, but there is a price to pay. Your images will be all over."

"OK."

"OK? That's it?"

"What do you want me to say?"

She takes a deep breath. "Let me give you some advice, Rook. Because if you like Ronin, and I know this from my own experience with Antoine, he will not want you to take those contracts. So if you do, you might pay that price too."

I take a swig of my beer and look away for a moment, over at Ronin and Antoine as they fool with the grill and the food. I'm not sure why, but this whole thing with Ronin is bugging me. "Elise, I like your brother. He's one sexy man, pardon me for saying that as you're his sister. And he's a model, and he's got a lot of money, but I've known the guy for four days. I'm not ready to base a life-changing decision off a potential relationship with him. So if you have a contract I'd like to read it and then I'd like to think about it."

Elise smiles, maybe for the first time since I got here. "Good girl. I was hoping you'd react like that. Ronin is my brother, but he's a twenty-two-year-old guy, you know? They are what they are, and something tells me you need stability right now, am I right?"

I nod. "Yes, I'd very much like to be stable."

"Well, twenty-two-year-old guys aren't known for their stability, if you get my meaning. Antoine was a lot older than me when we met and even then, it took me almost a year to trust him, so I get it." She lets out a deep breath and closes her eyes for an extended period of time. "It was very hard to trust that he would take care of me and to be perfectly honest, I still have panic attacks over it because we never married. So, think about it all very carefully." She pauses. "And if I could make one suggestion?"

"Yeah, sure."

"Be careful how much time you spend in Ronin's apartment. You have a place, I gave you that place, so use it. Please."

I think about this for a moment and it's like she's reading my mind.

"Yeah, OK."

Her face lights up. "Yeah?"

"I can see the wisdom in that. I crave some private space so bad, I can't even explain it."

She leans over and hugs me and then Ronin is up next to me. "What's going on? Girl hugs are a bad sign."

Chapter Twenty-Four

Ronin

Leave it to my sister to fuck everything up. Dammit. Rook is so skittish, she really is like a bird in that respect. Ready to take flight at the slightest hint that something is up. And can I blame her? If I had her past I'd be skittish too. Hell, I damn near did have her past and I am just barely recovered from it. It took Elise and me years to get over that shit.

But I do not want her down in the studio apartment.

We walk across the large lower terrace and I shake my head.

"What?" she asks.

"I just don't like the idea of you being down here alone. It's too far away, it's dark, it's creepy, it's—"

"It's four stories up and there's a keypad on the studio door."

I smile as I take her hand. She's brave. "I know, but it's far."

"Far from where?"

"Far from me, you little shit." She squeezes my hand

and I feel a little better because she's still sending some token I-like-you signals.

I open the door and find the light switch on the side of the wall, not ready to leave her yet.

"So what should I expect tomorrow?"

"Well," I say, trying my best not to ravish her mouth as I watch her chew on her lip. "If you sign the contract then we'll do a practice shoot, in private, well, semi-private. All the technicians will be there and probably two or three photographers."

"Why so many?"

"Antoine likes to get a bunch of angles, and he can only work one camera at a time, so he makes the other guys come in sometimes. Since we're planning on using you for TRAGIC, he'll want as many views as he can get."

"Will you be there with me? Or will I be alone?"

"I'll definitely be there, Gidget. We're submitting the two of us together for the contract."

"So I'll be naked with you?"

I tread carefully. "That's not quite how it works. It's all about the mood of the models."

She walks back to the bedroom and starts fixing the covers on the bed.

"Does that bother you?" I ask. "If I see your body?"

"I'm nervous," she confesses. "I've never done anything like this before, I'm not sure what to expect."

"Well, after tomorrow you'll know exactly what to expect. I won't let anything happen to you, OK?"

"OK," she says. "Thanks for walking me home and—" She stops abruptly. "Well, thanks for everything really."

I back away before I tackle her and rip that adorable little Gidget outfit right off her body. She catches me staring and smiles. "I'm on to you, Larue."

"Yeah," I say, closing the distance between us despite

my inner warnings. I wrap both hands around her hips and pull her a little closer. "I don't see how you're on to me when I'm innocent, I have nothing to hide."

"Well, I appreciate the Gidget outfit anyway. It's very cute. And I really expected you to come back with the blue nightie, so it was a huge step up in my mind."

I grin like an idiot picturing me dressing her up in that nightie and then taking her to dinner.

"Ah, I see your mind spinning with that thought. So, I appreciate your self-control in that area."

I back away again, because I see the stop sign she's getting ready to put up. "Tomorrow we'll do the cherry tree shoot. It will be completely different than what you experienced today, OK?"

"Well, that's if I sign the contract, right? I have to sign that first."

My eyes dart to the papers she set down in the nightstand and I have a moment of hope that she'll wake up in the morning and say screw this contract. But that will never happen, so I just exhale a long breath and force myself to smile. "Yeah, but I think you'll sign it, don't you?"

She studies me for a moment and her brows crease a little in thought. "I need the money," she says almost apologetically.

"Yeah, I get it."

"Well—"

"OK, goodnight, Rook." I turn and walk out of the garden apartment and make my way back upstairs. Maybe she *will* walk away from that contract tomorrow, who knows? I wish she would, because the minute she signs it I have to treat her like all the other models and I have a feeling she's not going to like that one bit.

Chapter Twenty-Five

After Ronin leaves I change into a pair of shorts and a t-shirt and slip into a long peaceful sleep. In fact, when I wake up in the morning I feel rested and at peace with my situation for the first time in like… forever. Even going all the way back to my childhood, before my mom overdosed and I went into foster care. She was a mess. Your typical teen mom. Broke, craving attention, no clue how to take care of a kid.

And my life was never peaceful. It was nothing but chaos. In fact, now that I think about it, my life has been one long chaotic episode after another.

When I first decided to put some thought into getting the hell away from my ex, Jon, I would go to the library and use their computer so I didn't have to worry about my browsing history being detected. I could never trust that anything I looked at on our home computer wasn't being traced because that was Jon's job. Computer forensics. He wasn't a cop but he worked with them all the time.

Scary shit if you're his ex-girlfriend trying to make a clean getaway.

Anyway, the library had all kinds of material on domestic abuse. It took me several visits to finally accept that was the situation I was in. Domestic abuse just sounded so clinical. I just knew he hit me, mostly for no reason, but sometimes I defied him on purpose just to make him do it and get it over with.

It turns out that men who abuse their partners go through a cycle—it starts out fine, then the tension builds and builds, he snaps and gets violent, and then the make-up stage is the only time he's reasonable.

So even though I didn't really understand this before reading that pamphlet, I could feel these phase changes. I could feel the anger and the tension building to a peak. And it drove me insane, how I had to just wait for him to release it. On me, of course. So sometimes I'd do something on purpose just to get to the make-up stage where I could relax for a few weeks.

Except there's just one problem with that rationale. After a period of time the abuse gets worse and worse and the make-up stage gets shorter and shorter until it fades away entirely. Then there's only tension and violence.

That's the stage Jon and I were in.

Twenty-four-hour tension and violence. If he wasn't hitting me he was yelling at me or calling me names. He especially liked 'whore,' even though he knew damn well he was the only man I'd ever been with. And the last time was the end of the line for me.

After that I knew he was going to kill me next time. Of course I could've called the police and stayed in Chicago, letting the system work it out. But the statistics were not in my favor. Most women went back and even if they did get a restraining order, the guys almost never respected it. There was even a pamphlet on the different methods the men would use to get the women back after incarceration or legal action.

I might still be pretty weak right now, but I am a hundred times stronger than I was back then. I know for sure—I'd have been one of those dumb girls who went back. I would've. So the only way out for me was escape to somewhere else.

I sigh and let all this bad stuff out with the air.

It's over now, so I can let it go. It's been months, he gave up, he's moved on and found someone else to beat, or maybe he got himself thrown in jail for hitting the wrong person. Whatever happened after I left, it didn't happen to me.

I smile at this even though I sorta feel guilty that I didn't put him away so he couldn't hurt anyone else. I am only one girl. And even now I'm not strong—just strong*er*—back then it was incomprehensible that I could do anything to stop him. Maybe someday I'll have it in me to fight back like that if it ever happens again, but right now I'm fragile.

But I'll take fragile. It's a hell of a lot better than broken.

And that's what I was back in Chicago. A mess of shattered emotions and irrational feelings that had no hope of understanding that what he did to me was not love.

That's the one thing I accepted pretty quick when I started to realize what was happening to me internally—the way I justified his acts and allowed him to keep me there in the house after his abuse. I was just as sick as him, but in a different way. I had a psychological disorder that grew over the years until I was incapable of understanding what a healthy relationship was.

I was sick. The abuse had conditioned me into some strange state of acceptance and I can remember every detail of the day it all became clear. I was sitting at a computer in the library and I suddenly looked around.

And asked myself an honest question.

Is this all there is for me?

I mean, I was a kid once. I had dreams. I had plans. But there I was. In a public library looking up facts about domestic violence when I had a state-of-the-art computer at home in my living room that I was afraid to use.

I was broken, beaten, and scared of pretty much everything.

And it hit me.

If I wanted to change my life then I'd have to do it myself. Because no one was coming to protect me, or save me, or heal me.

There was just me.

There is no such thing as heroes, no such thing as being rescued, and if I had a domestic violence problem, then I better be able to figure it out myself because if I didn't, I was going to end up dead.

And while Ronin seems like a good guy, he has triggered a lot of red flags that keep me guessing. And guessing about my safety isn't something I can afford to do right now. Because in the end there is still only me.

I need to keep this in mind as I make choices about what I will and won't do while I'm here living in Antoine Chaput's erotic photography studio.

Because if I'm not careful, the tide of abuse will wash over me again, and this time I might sink instead of swim.

Chapter Twenty-Six

Elise's knock disrupts my reality check and I smile at her face peeking in through the window next to the door. I trot over and let her in.

"OK, big day today, Rook. I've got a lot to tell you, so let's get started."

Elise is all business and I kind of like that because she seems like a straight shooter, she just lays it all out and steps back to let me react.

"I'm ready."

And I am. I listen to every word, she points out every single stipulation in the contract. Nowhere does it say I will take off my clothes, and nowhere does it say I can't refuse to do certain shots. I like this part. What it does say is that if I don't cooperate and allow the photographer to produce what he's asked to fulfill for the contract, I will not be paid. And if I don't follow the rules of conduct for the models, I will be fired and asked to leave.

It's my choice.

I initial each stipulation without blinking. I can do

this, I've decided. I will be cautious and think clearly and make decisions based on facts and not emotions. And the fact is that right now, I want that money. If I can get a few thousand dollars together, I can really make a go at starting again.

I'm not stupid—I know modeling is a short-term thing. This is not a career, just a stepping stone.

So I initial every stipulation and sign the contract.

Because I've thought about my second chance a lot over the past several months. I've dreamed it. I want it very badly. And for whatever reason the Chaput people have decided they want to help me get it. So I'm taking this chance and running with it until I'm out of breath. And when I've gotten all there is to get from it, I'm out and onto my own dreams.

Elise hugs me after my hand swishes the final letter of my name on the contract. "OK, Rook, let's go make some big money, shall we?"

"We shall," I say, laughing.

Elise and I walk into the studio together and I'm surprised at how calm things are compared to yesterday. She reads my expression. "Mondays are crazy," she explains. "We have to get all the contracts for the week settled and everyone is tense until the schedule is cemented. Most days are not like Monday, but they can be if we get something in that's on a short deadline."

She directs me to the salon chair and today we are the only ones, like it was last week when I first showed up. Has it only been five days since I met these people? Since I was homeless? Since I spent my last ten dollars on a coffee and had that little white card flipped at me in the coffee shop?

It can hardly be possible, but it is.

I have only really known Ronin for three days and change. The first day doesn't count because we never got a chance to talk until the day was over. He only said that one phrase about not making it here if they couldn't touch me when I first showed up.

Oh. God.

What am I doing?

Elise, the ever-perceptive older sister, picks up on my apprehension. "Take a deep breath. I'll be watching the whole thing, Rook. No one will take advantage of you here. I see everything."

I believe her and my heart rate calms.

"Besides," she says as she sprays water down the side of my face. "Ronin is your partner today, and I might be his sister, but it's hard not to notice. All the girls like him—"

I open my eyes and let some water splash in just so I can pay better attention to what she's saying.

"—*because*," she emphasizes, "he is very patient and gentle when the situation calls for it. He will take care of you while you're here modeling for us, trust me."

I relax and decide to go with it. I signed the contract, the money has been promised, the shoot is set up, I'm getting my hair done, and Ronin's hands are the ones that will be on me, not some stranger's.

That sends shivers all the way up my body.

Elise adjusts the water temperature, thinking I'm cold, and I decide that she really does see everything.

When Elise is done I change into a thin wraparound robe that ties in the front. She styles my hair straight, then braids it loosely so that it falls down the front of me. She paints on some make-up while another girl removes the cherry-red polish on my nails that was just applied yesterday and exchanges it for a pale pink.

When they turn my chair around so I can see myself in the mirror I'm a little taken back. "I thought the theme was tragic? I look… sweet."

Not at all how I imagined.

"Well, this is pretty much how tragedy takes hold, right, Rook? You start out all sweet and innocent and then bam, your world is ripped apart. So for this shoot you are happy and yes, sweet. I have your clothes set out in the dressing room, you won't have to worry about your hair, it's a zip-up."

And that's my cue to get up and get ready. My stomach is a ball of knots as I make my way into the dressing room. There's only one garment bag on the rack and it's got a slip of paper on it that says, ROOK—TRAGIC.

"Ready?" Ronin's husky voice whispers down into my neck as his hands brush against my shoulders for a moment, then take hold and turn me around.

"Yeah, I think so."

"OK, first things first. I need you to step on the scale." He points to a large stand-up scale in the corner. It looks like it belongs in a doctor's office.

"Why?"

He raises his eyebrow at me.

"I mean, why do you need to weigh me?"

He pushes on the small of my back and guides me over to the scale. "Because, Rook, this is my job here. I run the girls, I run the closet, and I take it very seriously. So now that the contract is signed, I have to keep track of you. Please, step on the scale."

I think I feel sick. He gets to weigh me? "What if I

don't?"

"Why do you care if I weigh you?" he asks with an annoyed look on his face.

"It's degrading. You're reducing me to a number."

"It's not just a number, it's an indicator."

I turn as my whole body goes hot with anger. "Indicator of *what*?"

"Of whether or not you are following the rules we have in place for keeping the models looking a certain way."

He waits as I process what he just said and then reads my silence as acceptance and pushes me until I step on the scale. He steps around to the other side and writes the number down in a tablet. I can't see the number because it's hidden from this side.

"Well?"

"Well, what?" he asks, pushing me to move off the scale and shaking the garment bag at me.

"How much do I weigh?"

"It's just a number, Rook. I never tell the girls how much they weigh."

"Why not? It seems pretty stupid to weigh people and then keep it a secret if you ask me."

"Because I'm not interested in what you weigh, only in whether or not you change from the weight you are now."

I snatch the bag from him and walk away. I am so fucking glad I did not decide to rely on Ronin Flynn, because he's an asshole. I choose the same dressing room as I did yesterday and unzip the bag to look at the clothes.

It's a pink knee-length dress and it's straight out of Gidget. I stand on my tip toes and peek over the door.

Ronin smiles and waves his finger at me from down the hall.

There's no underwear or bra again.

I slip out of my clothes and pull the dress on. It's got a squared-off neckline that plunges right down to my girls and a wire underneath so they are pushed up high on my chest.

So I guess I'm skanky Gidget today.

"There's no shoes," I call out.

"Just go barefoot," Ronin says, peeking over the door at me.

"Do you mind?"

He responds by opening the door and stepping into the dressing room with me. "Turn around," he says, twirling his finger at me. "I'll zip you up."

Oh. I turn and he zips. "I thought you were shooting with me?"

"I am."

"Then how come you're not dressed?"

"I am."

"You're wearing jeans and a t-shirt, like you always do."

"Rook, no one gives a shit what I wear. They want me naked and if I'm not naked, then I'm just there to make you look good until we do get naked."

My face has got to be scarlet red. "Oh."

"Ready then?"

"Ready as I'll ever be, I guess." Ronin takes my hand and leads me out to the terrace and when I step over that threshold I feel it in my bones. Nothing about my life will ever be the same after this. I'm just not sure if that's a good or bad thing just yet.

Chapter Twenty-Seven

I am lost in my own thoughts as Ronin leads me across the terrace to the cherry trees. Antoine and Elise are sitting at one of the picnic tables, chatting and smiling. There is no one else around, not even a light person. This makes me let out a long exhale and Ronin squeezes my hand. "You OK?" he asks, stopping for a moment to get my response.

"Yeah, I'm just glad there's not a lot of people around."

"I set it up that way, Rook. Just let me take care of things now, OK?"

I nod so he'll drop it, but this control stuff with him is really setting me back. He acts like I'm not allowed to question him.

We've reached Antoine and Elise now and they are talking, both to me and to Ronin, but I just nod my head and agree because I have no idea what they're talking about. Technical stuff. Natural light, Antoine says. I look around and yes, sure enough, the sun is shining right into the middle of the cherry trees on the east side of the terrace.

I study the 'set' and notice that the swing I was sitting in the other night is not even attached to the tree branches, it's attached to a long green pole that spans the entire grove. There's a picnic set up on the grass, complete with wine glasses, cheese, and a bowl of cherries. The blanket isn't checkered though, it's a crisp white with cotton lace on the edges, and there are cherry blossom petals all over the place. I'm not sure if that was planned or not, because each time the wind blows, those boughs, heavy with the sweet-smelling flowers, release dozens of them at a time.

Everything about these trees says climax. The flowers are mature, falling off and getting ready for the tree to bear fruit over the summer. It's a single moment in time that will be captured on digital film for eternity.

And I'm part of that.

I get the chills and Ronin, still talking to Antoine and Elise, absently pulls me closer to him, like he senses my needs and wants to keep me warm.

It's all very confusing. I like that he notices when I'm having a problem and need something, but I don't like relying on him for stuff and I hate the fact that he's allowed to make decisions for me. It's too personal.

But that's what this contract is all about though, isn't it? I've basically given them my body in exchange for money. And I just have to trust that they will not take advantage of me.

They are finished with their conversation and Ronin leads me over to the cherry tree and leans up against the smooth bark of the trunk and then puts his hands on my hips. We are not that close, there's a good eight inches between us, but I can feel his heat and his hands instantly warm the skin under my dress.

"You OK?" he asks.

"Yeah, I'm good. So what's the plan?" I nod my head over at the blanket. "Besides the picnic?"

"We're gonna get some straight couples shots right here against the tree. We gotta be quick to catch the light just right though, because Antoine likes natural light." He stops to nod at Antoine and the camera shutter begins to click as Ronin continues to talk. "And then we'll just have a little romantic picnic. Sound good?"

"OK, but what do I do? I don't get it."

"Just what you're doing right now, Gidget." He smiles at my new nickname and I blush a little. "See, that right there is what Antoine is looking for. An honest reaction to the situation. So I'll flirt with you and you react. That's pretty much it."

"I think I can handle that."

"Good," he says as his grip on my hips tightens and he pulls me into him. His hands sneak around behind me, not quite on my ass, but not quite *not* on my ass either. They are hovering just on the edge of inappropriate behavior.

Of course, I signed up for this so he's already got permission. I swallow and pull my upper body back as he continues to bring us closer.

"Relax, Gidge. I've got you."

I do, I relax and he pushes my pelvis against his groin. I look up quickly and he's almost laughing at me. The shutter is still clicking away as Antoine moves around us. He speaks to Ronin, but it's all in French, so I have no idea what he's saying and Ronin doesn't reply or translate for me. His attention is one hundred percent on my face, watching everything I do, searching my eyes for questions, his hands still hovering just at the edge of sexy as they caress my hips, then move down a few inches and return.

It's not so bad really.

Shit, who the hell am I kidding? Ronin Flynn's hands on my ass feel spectacular. I grin up at him and he smiles.

"Good, now let's move on to the next shot, OK?"

"What's—"

I stop mid-sentence because his mouth is nuzzling into my neck, his breath hot as it sweeps up into my ear, making me shudder and let out a little moan. "You OK?"

"Mmmmhmmmm," is all I can manage, because a chill rockets down my spine and my head involuntarily tips back and gives him permission to suck on my neck.

Holy shit.

He pulls back for a moment, just long enough to say, "Touch me, Rook," and then his mouth is back on my neck. He takes my left hand, which has a firm grasp on one of his belt loops, a safe move if ever there was one, and flattens my palm against his waist. I move the other hand in a feeble attempt to be an active participant instead of a dead fish who only reacts.

"More of that and we can put this scene to rest."

I take a deep breath and slip my hand under his t-shirt and then we both let a little gasp together as the chills travel up his body now. Antoine is talking in French again and Ronin leans down and takes my mouth.

It's a soft kiss at first, but as soon as I open up for his tongue his hands go behind my neck and it turns into something way beyond soft. He crushes my mouth with his, drawing in a breath that says he's absolutely turned on. This excites me and I kiss him back with just as much force, our tongues probing and twisting, our breath coming in gasps and long draws, like there is not enough air in the world to fuel this kiss. His hands are all over my body now, one still grasping the back of my neck to keep me close to him, the other, the one not on the side where Antoine is clicking away at the camera, slips under my skirt and travels up my thigh.

I moan and then catch Elise moving in out of the corner of my eye and Ronin withdraws his secret hand, bringing it out in full view once again.

"Take my shirt off." It's not a sweet request, it's a command. For like a fraction of a millisecond I wonder if he's allowed to command me, but I slap that cautious Rook away and do what I'm told.

"Slow?" I ask him.

"As long as you drag your fingers up my body as you do it, slow is just fine with me."

Oh fuck!

I take the thin fabric between my fingertips and slide my palms against his body as I lift and then roll it up, inch by inch. I'm driving him crazy, I can tell, mostly because he's practically biting my ear and whispering, "You're driving me fucking crazy, Gidget." I only make it up to his chest before he releases his hold on my neck and whips the shirt over his head in one sweeping motion, then bunches it up in front of him and throws it over at Elise who is still standing guard off to the side where the offending hand was wandering a few minutes ago.

Antoine barks in French again and then Ronin pulls back and leads me over to the blanket.

"Lie down," he says in that throaty command he gave earlier.

I'll debate whether or not I should be putting up with that later, but right now, I'm all in. I kneel down, smooth my dress out a little and then lie back on the cool cotton blanket. My skin is so hot and feverish from the kisses and touching that the blanket soothes me. Everything around me smells like cherry blossoms, and when I turn my head I realize that they are all over the blanket now because Elise swoops in to adjust my hair and place the flowers in strategic locations. Ronin is messing with the food and pouring the wine into glasses.

And before I know what's happening he's lying down next to me, leaning down and pressing himself over my stomach. I sigh at the dress, because it's the only thing separating my bare skin from his. "Just a few shots like this, Rook, then we'll sit up and have some fun." He's got a devilish grin as the words come out.

"Finally," I say with mock exasperation. "I'm starting to get bored."

He growls down at me and then goes back to kissing my neck so he can whisper in my ear, "I'd have you naked by now if Elise wasn't here."

"Ohhh, you're being bad," I whisper back, being equally discreet. "I bet she grounds you if I tell her what you just said."

We stare at each other for a few seconds, his eyes searching me for a moment. "Date me, Rook."

"What?"

"Let me take you out."

I look over at Elise who is distracted by an assistant who has joined us. "Are we allowed?"

"Pffft." He rolls off me and sits up, then pulls me up and sets me on his lap. I'm breathless with the quick change of position and almost gasp when he leans in to whisper in my ear again. "Pay close attention, Gidget." And then Antoine is giving orders and Ronin is fixing my dress so that it flares out around his legs.

It occurs to me then… I have no fucking underwear on.

And the reason it occurs to me is because his

excitement is right underneath my completely bare girly parts.

Antoine is on Ronin's left, so Ronin's left hand begins to caress my foot with small circles, a touch so light it actually makes me squirm because my feet are totally ticklish. He takes the hint and slowly sweeps up my calf, which is just about the most sensual feeling I've ever experienced. I moan out a little and his bruising kisses are back, crushing against my mouth.

Just as Antoine takes his attention to our lips Ronin's right hand also begins at my foot, swirling his fingertips around the soft pad of my arch. I laugh into his mouth and he pulls me close, my hair hiding our faces for a moment, and says, "Shhhh, now. Be good, Gidge." And then his right hand sweeps up my leg and under my dress, caressing the same small circles along my inner thigh.

"Oh, shit," I whimper as I bury myself in his neck. Just a few more inches and I'm going to come undone. My neck tilts back as the sensations all crash together and he takes his kisses to my plunging neckline, his left hand, the one still out in the open, slips up to my breast just as the hidden hand drops down a little farther, just a flutter of a touch against my crease.

He reaches over, not with the hidden hand, and picks up a glass of wine and hands it to me.

My fingertips barely understand what to do with the glass because the only thing on my mind is where his other hand is. We each take a sip and then he bites into a cherry, taking half of it in his mouth, and spits out the pit.

Antoine barks something harsh in French and Ronin laughs. "It's a fucking pit, Antoine, it's not *litter*." He rolls his eyes at me. "Sit still now, Rook, and keep your mouth closed for a moment."

My mind is still on his fingers as they caress my inner

thigh, but I do my best not to squirm.

He brings the cherry to my lips and I keep my mouth closed. This makes him smile and then he traces my lips, dripping juice as he paints them. I'm just about to let my tongue dart out and get the juice when Ronin's mouth reaches up and licks it off, stopping to suck on my bottom lip, and then gives it a little nibble that makes me cry out.

He bites into another cherry and again, to Antoine's disgust, woofs out the pit into the grass. Spitting is a skill only boys really acquire. They are so good at it. It might gross out Antoine, but not me. I think just about everything Ronin is doing with his mouth is astonishing right now. The secret hand under my dress appears again. He lifts my left hand and paints each fingertip pad with cherry juice, then sucks it off, nibbling them one by one, just like he did my lips.

I just stare at him and his eyes never leave mine. "What?" he finally asks.

"You—" I say.

He raises his eyebrows.

"—are bad."

He laughs. "If you were naked right now I'd drip this juice all down your belly and let my tongue—"

"OK, that's enough," Antoine says. "Excellent job, Rook."

Fucking Antoine.

I bite my lip as Ronin licks my fingertips one more time and then grins up at me like an idiot. "Want to come over and watch a movie, Gidget?"

I nod enthusiastically as Elise helps me up, and then Ronin bounces to his feet and puts his arm around me protectively. "You fell asleep pretty quick last time, are you sure you're up for a movie?"

I'm not sure if a movie is the code word for sex or not right now, but either way, I'm definitely up for it.

Chapter Twenty-Eight

Ronin

"Hold on, stud!" Elise calls out before I can swoop Rook back inside and up to my apartment.

"Go change and I'll meet you outside the dressing room, OK?"

Rook nods and walks off and I watch her until the glass doors close behind her and she turns the corner. I turn back to my meddling sister who is already shaking her head at me. "What? That was some shoot, eh? Don't you think? She's perfect. I can't wait till tomorrow." I laugh a little because while I really am excited for tomorrow, I know mentioning it like this is pissing Elise off.

Bad.

"You are not dating that girl, Ronin. I mean it. She belongs to the studio for now—when this contract is up, you two can talk about having babies and all that shit. But for now, you stay out of her pants, do you hear me?"

"I'm offended, Elise. Really. I'm a professional."

She eyes me cautiously for several long seconds. "If

you do, I'll know. And I will be pissed, do you understand?"

"It's a movie, Elise. I'm gonna feed her some more fruit and get her a little drunk, what could possibly go wrong?"

"I'm not kidding. I saw your little stealth hand move, by the way. Next time I'll pull the plug, but Antoine is exhausted tonight so I ignored it." She stops to glare at me. "I won't ignore it again. And she's not even legal, Ronin. You will *not* get her drunk."

"Would you relax, Ellie! It was a joke, since when do I get minors drunk? Fuck, I don't know why you're going all batshit about this. I'm gonna take care of her just like I take care of all the rest, except I'm gonna enjoy our photoshoots just a little bit more than usual." I grin, thinking that remark is fantastically fun in my mind, but Elise is not amused.

"That's what I'm concerned with, Ronin. We don't need another Mardee on our hands."

Oh... buuuuurn. What a bitch. "You know what? Fuck you, Elise. I was nineteen fucking years old when she came through here. I had no idea what she was doing."

"And that's my point, dumbass. This girl is nineteen too, she's had some kind of very recent upheaval in her life, and you're fucking with her head right now. Stay out of her pants, do you understand? Or I will pull you from this project so fast your dick will spin."

"Whatever." I wave her off and go back inside. I am not responsible for Mardee, that's one thing I've come to terms with since all that shit went down. I could no more have stopped her than anyone else. And Elise insinuating that I dropped the ball when she was modeling for us just pisses me off.

Rook is already dressed when I get back inside. She's waiting by the door, biting her lip.

"What?" I ask, a little impatiently as I direct her up the stairs.

"What was that about?"

"Nothing, don't worry about it."

"I put the dress back in the bag and hung it up on the rack."

I shake Elise's words off and take my attention back to Gidget as we round the corner and head to my apartment door. "Perfect, I'll take care of it in the morning. Are you still up for a movie?"

She nods. "Yeah, sure."

Rook is not Mardee, in fact, Rook is the anti-Mardee. There is not one thing I can think of that might link the two. They don't look alike, they certainly don't act alike, and I never thought of Mardee as anything more than a fun interlude between girlfriends.

And she thought the same of me. We were mutually apathetic towards each other.

"But Elise didn't look too happy."

I push Rook inside the apartment and close the door, then take her face in my hands. "Who cares?" I kiss her again but she's not as interested as she was down on the terrace. "She's just overprotective, that's all. She worries about the girls, especially the ones I date." I stop here to make a point. "But I'd just like you to know, I don't bring them home, Rook. Ever."

She shoots me an incredulous look.

"I swear, I'm not saying I'm celibate or anything, but I don't bring them here to this apartment."

"So where do you take them?"

"It's a four-story building and we're the only people who live here. There are lots of places downstairs."

"Oh," is all she says to that and I take a deep breath, feeling stupid for admitting that I fuck girls in random rooms in our building.

"You have to be hungry, are you?" I ask, trying to change the subject.

She pushes me away from her, then ducks under my arm, walks into the living room and takes a seat on the couch. "I am. What do you have?"

Yeah, that moment during the photoshoot is pretty much gone. I go into the kitchen and open the fridge. "Fruit," I call. "Apples, Cuties, grapes, and pomegranate seeds."

"That's quite a selection," she says from behind me.

I spin around, surprised. "I love fruit. I blame it on Antoine. He gets fruit baskets delivered every week. I'm not even sure where they come from, like maybe he's got a subscription to one of those Fruit of the Week Clubs or something? I'm not sure. But for the last dozen years or so I've been eating fresh fruit out of a basket that sits on Antoine's desk in his office."

She's smiling again and my heart lifts. Maybe I didn't fuck it up?

"You've never asked where they come from?"

"Nope."

"Why? If you've always wondered."

"Because it's gonna be something stupid like Mamie Chaput or the fucking Fruit of the Week Club. And I'd rather imagine something more exotic, like maybe it comes from some long lost love who lives in Fiji—and she misses Antoine so much, she sends him fruit every week to remind him of what they might've had?"

"You have a Mamie Chaput?"

I laugh. "Yeah, well, Antoine is French, in case you haven't noticed. I kinda got sucked into the family by extension."

"Wouldn't that be weird for Elise if there *was* some woman sending Antoine fruit baskets every week?"

"Yeah, probably. But I like picturing this girl in a string bikini, lying in the sun on a tropical island, pining over the one that got away. I never said it was practical, just exotic."

I hand her a Cutie and take out a container of pom seeds for me.

"So all you eat at home is fruit?" she asks, looking at my fridge.

"Nah, I eat everything, but I never go grocery shopping, so I just steal fruit from the baskets downstairs."

"But you have beer?" she adds, looking at the many different Colorado microbrews I have stashed in the fridge.

I grin at her. "OK, enough of your questions. Go eat your orange."

"So you make it to the liquor store and the fruit basket, but that's it? And you don't bring girls up here, but you do take them to some hidden harem room downstairs?"

I'm not sure if she's joking at this point.

"That's some picture you've painted in my head, Ronin."

I take her orange back and start peeling. The sooner she can eat it, the sooner she stops psychoanalyzing me. "That's not the picture I want you to have at all, Rook. I'm just your typical twenty-two-year-old guy."

"OK," she says, taking the orange back half-peeled. "I get it."

"Get what?" Somehow this whole day has turned against me and I'm not quite sure where it all went wrong.

"I wasn't sending any messages, so I'm not sure what you get."

She hands the orange back and walks away.

"What?"

I let out a deep breath as the front door closes.

And I sit on the couch, absently flipping through channels, wondering how the fuck I just blew this whole day with a conversation about fruit baskets.

Chapter Twenty-Nine

OK.

I'm certifiably stupid for just walking out over a fruit basket, but it's not about the fruit. It's about Elise's warnings. Both the one she gave me last night and the one she just gave Ronin downstairs. I only caught part of it, and maybe I don't know who Mardee is, but whatever happened to her, Elise thinks Ronin was the cause and Ronin was immediately defensive.

I'm no shrink, but I'm guessing that defensiveness comes up when you're playing defense. Which means he had something to do with the bad thing that happened to this Mardee girl, regardless of what he says.

I head straight for the door and skip down the stairs to get my own food from Cookie's. There's no baseball game today and lunch is technically over, so the streets are fairly quiet. I walk the block over to the diner in thought, then tell the hostess inside that "I belong to Ronin" and head back to the table. It's empty so I sink into the booth and grab a menu sitting behind the salt and pepper shakers.

Elise also said I needed stability and maybe Ronin doesn't fit that criteria. I think that bothers me a little more after he got all personal in the photoshoot than it did before. Before the shoot we were just flirting, but his hand went beyond flirting today. And then there was the little remark about Elise being protective of the girls he dates.

Why?

I mean, I don't consider us dating, but beyond that—why does Elise need to feel protective towards the girls he dates?

I order a salad and watch people as I wait. This place is still pretty busy for being almost three o'clock. A guy comes in who catches my eye. Not because he's hot, even though he is hot, but because from the minute he comes through the door he's watching me. I look behind me just to make sure, but there are no people dining behind me. He takes his attention to the hostess. He's got short messy hair, not quite blond, but not really brown either, and a little bit of facial hair. Enough to make him look rough, but not unkempt. The waitress points back to me and I watch the hot guy smile.

What the hell?

He starts walking towards me and once the counter is out of the way, it's hard to miss the fact that he's a biker. He's got the tell-tale biker boots on and they sound off a manly thud on the polished concrete floors as he approaches my booth. When he pushes up the sleeves on his white thermal I see what else he's got. Tattoos all over. Like everywhere.

He stops right in front of the booth and smiles down at me.

"Let me guess," I say sarcastically, "you belong to

Ronin?"

He slides into the booth across from me and laughs. "Hey, if it gets me a seat here with you, I'll belong to that dickhead for an hour." He offers his hand. "Spence."

"Rook," I offer back as I shake his hand.

"Yeah, I figured. Antoine described you on the phone, but shit, he really played you down. You're perfect."

I twist my eyebrows at him. "Perfect for—?" and that's when Ronin walks into the diner. The hostess points back to us, but he doesn't need an invitation, he's already halfway down the aisle. I watch him very carefully, but whatever his deal is, it's got nothing to do with me because his eyes are blazing at my new dining companion.

"Spencer Shrike, what the fuck are you doing sitting in my booth talking to one of my girls?"

Oh, really! If these asshole men weren't about to throw in the diner I would be so offended at that comment!

Spencer Shrike gets to his feet and claps Ronin on the back. "Good to see you too, asshole. Now sit the fuck down. You know too fucking well I'm here on business. And now that I've met Rook, I'm more convinced than ever you guys deserve the STURGIS contract."

Ronin motions for me to move over and pushes on my upper arm a little to make me hurry. I shoot him a dirty look as I scoot, but he ignores me. "Rook has a job, sorry. I've already set up Bonnie and Val for you to try out tomorrow."

Spencer takes his attention to me as my salad arrives. We all sit back and shut up until the waitress leaves, but then Spence picks it up right where it left off. "Is that so, Rook? You're booked up through August?"

"August? I have no idea," I admit. "When does this

job end, Ronin?"

Ronin growls and it takes all my self-control not to spit out a crouton as I laugh. Oh, shit. He might start pissing on me soon.

I shake my head. "I highly doubt I'll be busy until August. Is this another modeling job?" I take another bite of salad and chew methodically as I watch the silent bro-down going on at the table.

"She's busy," Ronin says through clenched teeth.

"I'm not busy, Ronin. Let the man speak."

Spencer smiles and then scoots down his booth bench so he's across from me again. "It's a complicated deal, Rook, but I'd love for you to attend the meeting I have with Antoine in about," he checks his phone, "thirty minutes. You in?"

"How much does it pay?"

"Not set in stone, so don't worry about that. We've got studio money behind us for this job," now he's talking to Ronin, "so think about that before you turn into a Neanderthal, Flynn. Can I expect to see you in the meeting?"

His blue eyes track back to me and I shrug. "Sure, what do I have to lose?"

Spencer Shrike slips on some very dark sunglasses and shoots me with his finger. "See you then, Blackbird."

I smile at the nickname. A rook is a blackbird over in Europe. Not many people know that. Most of them think I'm named after a chess piece.

Ronin catches my pleasure and even though every defense mechanism left over from my previous life tells me to hide that smile to avoid a confrontation, I don't. I flash it even bigger, daring Ronin to make a big deal about getting my pants charmed off by a biker.

I take another bite of my salad and then Ronin gets

up and follows Spencer out the door, leaving me alone.

I show up fifteen minutes late for the meeting. On purpose. I figure they're all in there acting like dicks and that's not something I need to be a part of. Chaput Studios might own me for the TRAGIC contract, but I highly doubt this thing lasts for three months, so there's no way they can stop me from doing this STURGIS job if I really want to. It's best to just let the men-folk fight that out in private, come back to reality when they figure out none of them are in control, I am, and then settle back down in the world I live in.

The one where I call my own shots.

I knock softly and Ronin opens the door.

There are like ten people in the room, some suits, some bikers, and of course, Ronin, Antoine, and Elise. It doesn't take a genius to understand the STURGIS contract is about bikes. Obviously the only thing associated with Sturgis is bikers. So this should be interesting. I'm game, that's for sure.

Everyone goes silent as I enter, then Antoine takes over.

"Sit, Rook. Spence invited you, so you're welcome to listen in, but there will be no model negotiations for this meeting."

I almost do shut up and sit down, because that's basically what Antoine just told me to do. But that's dumb. "Well, I'm not about to sit in on a tense meeting when it has nothing to do with me, so if I'm not going to be provided with any useful information, I'll just take off."

They all stare at me.

Spencer stands and takes control. "Rook, we're going

to offer you the contract. I've been told that TRAGIC wraps up next week..."

Next week? That was quick. I figured this job would last a little longer than that. Ronin was not kidding about modeling being erratic. I think I might actually *need* this job.

"... so we'll talk more then."

Wait—what did I just miss? Everyone is looking at me, waiting for an answer, and I break into a sweat. "OK, yeah, sure. I'll leave you guys to it then." I pull the door closed behind me and go back to my apartment, still thinking about how quick I could be homeless again. I mean, this is their place, I'm no one, just another model among hundreds who have probably come through here, and they are letting me stay here because I have a contract with them.

Which will run out next freaking week!

I plop down on my couch and watch TV for a while, my gaze absently wandering to the front window, waiting to see if Ronin will come by for a visit tonight.

But he doesn't.

And I don't blame him.

Because I was a total bitch today.

I bite my lip and watch RetroTube until Gidget comes on. And that just makes everything worse, because even though I've been trying to talk myself out of it for the past week, I think I might actually like Ronin Flynn.

I wake early the next morning. Elise came by late last night and told me to be downstairs at seven AM, so I make my way into the studio ten minutes early to find everyone is already working. It still amazes me the early schedule these people keep. The dressing room is buzzing with girls. And every single one of them is naked.

I'm not talking topless, I'm talking *naked.*

They are chatting and laughing and generally acting like being nude is just another day on the job. And I guess it is when you work here.

I stand there a little lost when I hear Ronin's call.

"Over here, Gidget. Get on the scale and then Elise wants you in the salon for hair and make-up."

I forgot about the fucking scale.

Ronin doesn't smile at me, in fact, he barely notices me as I walk over to him. I step on the scale and I'm about to say something to break our awkward silence when a girl storms in, fully clothed and looking like she never went home from a party the night before, screaming at Ronin in French.

Ronin walks away and takes the girl by the arm, trying to shove her out of the dressing room. It's only then that I recognize her. The screamer from the day I came for my test shoot.

Clare.

Ronin's voice rises with hers and they stand toe to toe, yelling right up in each other's face. She pushes Ronin and he spins her around and drags her out into the studio, where her French threats echo off the tall ceilings.

"Fucking Clare," a naked blonde girl huffs out next to me.

"I know," another naked girl, this time a redhead, says with disgust. "I don't care who that bitch is, I'm glad Ronin canned her ass. She thinks she can break the rules, do whatever she wants, and still have a job?" The blonde girl snorts at this. "No," Red answers herself emphatically. "She's under his thumb just like we are. Right, Rook?" She smiles over at me.

"Whose thumb?"

"Ronin's, of course. Unless, you two have some deal going." She narrows her eyes at me.

"What deal?"

"Well, I find it interesting that you got the garden apartment and don't have to be at work on time. Why is that? Ronin keeping you or something?"

"What does that even mean?"

They laugh and go back to their clothes and it's only then that I notice every girl in the dressing room is staring at me. "What?" I ask them.

They turn back to their business but I'm left there feeling stupid so I just turn on my heel and go find Elise in the salon.

Thankfully things in the salon seem a little more

amicable. I don't generally care if the girls I work around are friends with me or not—typically when I have a job I'm there to work, not socialize. But that blonde girl asked if Ronin was *keeping me.* And Elise said something very similar the other night when we had dinner with her and Antoine. She said, *You're not any different from the other models, just because Ronin wants to keep you.*

What the fuck does that mean?

I'm not sure but the alarms are going off in my head again. I could let it slip by as a cute way to say he likes me, but now this girl said it too. Not to mention the whole *I belong to Ronin* thing they have going on down at the diner.

"Over here, Rook." Elise points to the shampoo chair and I ease back, ready to relax for a moment, even if it is in a shampoo chair and I just woke up an hour and a half ago.

It takes several hours for them to make me up, not so much because what they're doing to me is complicated, but because there are so many girls here today they have to keep trading us off like an assembly line. One does toes, one does hands, one does hair, one does make-up.

It's total insanity.

But I kinda like it. Everything goes fast, people are talking fast, walking fast, the girls come and then they go. The photographers are busy calling out directions, the camera shutters are clicking wildly.

It's all very exciting.

Everything I imagined a big important photography studio would be. Before I came here and found out it wasn't, of course. But today it's all business. After Ronin gets rid of that Clare chick, no one has time to think about anything but doing their job. Finally, when it's well past lunch, Elise pronounces me ready and ushers me off to the dressing room to get dressed, then tells me to meet them all out on the terrace.

I head into the dressing room, which is eerily quiet compared to the chaos I just came from, and find my clothes on the rack. Ronin is nowhere to be found and for a minute I miss him being there for me. He's not been around all day. The girls gossiped about him all morning though, talking about Clare.

I'm getting the impression she was an ex-girlfriend.

It bugs me that I feel jealous over that, but I really haven't had time to think about it much.

I lift the bag of clothes off the rack, expecting it to weigh—something—but it's like air. Like that bag contains almost nothing. I walk over to the armless couches that span the middle of the room and open it up.

It's a men's dress shirt. White.

And a pair of little boxer shorts that were definitely not made for a man.

It takes me two seconds to put the new clothes on. I button the shirt all the way up, then feel a little stupid and unbutton three of them.

Even though the shirt drops down to my mid-thigh, is long-sleeved, and goes up to my neck—I feel exposed. I exhale a long breath and force myself to walk out into the studio. Ronin is the first face I see because he's standing in the doorway as I turn the corner that hides the dressing room from onlookers.

He smiles and all the tension just evaporates.

"You're so fucking sexy."

I actually blush at that.

He takes my hand and leads me over to the terrace, then opens the door and waves me through like a gentleman.

There are about a dozen people outside and the afternoon sun is shining down on the terrace. It's shedding a lovely pink light and I can only assume that Antoine is in love with how it drapes over everything, washing out the drab harshness of the city and making it all soft.

Once I'm noticed everyone snaps to attention and then lights are on and those black umbrella things they use for diffusing it come out, and people are all busy. Ronin leads me over to a nook in the side of the building. There's a flowering cherry tree in a massive pot in the middle of the nook and the branches reach out and soft pink petals brush my cheek as I follow him under the canopy. "This is where we're shooting today, OK?"

All the camera shutters start clicking and I look over at the photographers.

Ronin directs my gaze back to him with a light touch on my chin. "I'm right here, Gidge. Forget about them, understand? You're not posing for them, you are reacting to me today. OK?"

I nod.

"They will not interfere unless it's time to stop. Otherwise you will only look at me or where I tell you to look. Ignore them completely. They do not exist."

"OK," I say, gulping down some air. That makes all the cameras start clicking again and it takes all my self-control not to look over at them.

"Good girl," Ronin says smiling. "Now, let me explain the rules. We both have power here. I have power to tell you what to do, to make you react, and to get the shots we need. Does that makes sense?"

"Yes, you're here to help me give them what they want."

"Yes, that's a good way to put it. I take care of you in the shoot, Rook, but my hands will be all over your body. Are you going to be OK with that?" I nod. "Words, please," he prods.

"Yes, I'm OK with that."

"And if the situation calls for it, meaning if we're getting the reactions we need, if everything is working, I might undress you."

"Might?"

"We make art here, Rook. We want the models to exhibit feelings that can be felt immediately when people see the pictures—we are not making porn."

"OK." More clicking shutters almost make me look but instead I find Ronin's eyes and ask him instead. "Why are they shooting already?"

"Because today is the first time you've ever done this and right now you're looking very sweet and innocent." He grins and wraps one hand around my waist, pulling me into him. The cameras go wild again. "Your reaction right now, as we do this for the first time, is priceless."

I blush and try hard to tuck the smile away, but I fail and try and forget about the cameras. They're doing their job, Ronin is doing his job, and I need to do mine.

Which is, as far as I can tell from yesterday's fully clothed version of a shoot, letting Ronin make me feel good.

"OK, now on to your power. You can give me direction in how quickly I proceed. Fast is not generally something we want. We want to make it all slow so the photographers can get their shots. But sometimes we get going and things move too fast, or maybe you're feeling uncomfortable. When that happens you can tell me one of two things. If you say the word *slow*, I'll change direction until you're comfortable again."

"OK, slow. Got it. What's the other one?"

"You can tell me to *stop*. And then the shoot ends and we all go home. Understand that, when you say stop, the shoot ends. So use it when you want things to be over. Not because you want things to change direction. Use slow for that, OK?"

He slips his hands under my shirt and caresses the skin just above the waistband of my shorts and while I know the cameras are clicking, suddenly I stop hearing them. My focus is one hundred percent on Ronin. His touch sends shivers up my entire body and my nipples perk to attention.

He smiles, like he knows, but he can't possibly know. The shirt is big and there's no way to see them.

Still he grins like he knows.

"Now, there's one more thing you can tell me." His hands retreat and start undoing the lower buttons of the shirt. He stops at the button just below my breasts and then returns his hands to my waist, but this time he pulls the shirt back, exposing my belly in the process. He looks down at my little boxer shorts.

"I love those," he whispers before looking back up at my face. He licks his lower lip. My tongue darts out and mimics him before I can stop it.

"What's the other thing I can tell you?"

He leans down to my neck and kisses me softly. I know the cameras are going crazy, but all I hear is his breath in my ear. Heat fills my lower body and I have to inhale deeply, making my whole chest rise and then fall with my exhale.

"The other thing you can tell me is *go*, Gidget." His hand wraps around my neck and massages my jaw line with his thumb while his words tickle all the way into my ear canal. I swallow down the desire that's building in me. "When you're done with slow, you tell me to go."

His mouth pulls away from my neck and finds my face. He's so close our lips almost touch, my mouth opens a little in anticipation and his hand glides up my torso and tenderly grabs my breast.

And then his mouth is on mine, his tongue flicking in, his mouth closing, then another flick. I close my eyes and my head drifts back a little as I respond. He's pinching my nipples now, ever so slightly, just enough to know his fingers are on me, are in control of me.

He teases me with his kiss over and over. I let him at first, I let him control me with his movements, his hands still drifting up and over my breasts, a little more forcefully now.

But then the desire inside me takes over and I reach up and wrap my hands around his neck, I pull him to me, I let my fingertips glide down his chest. He's bare on top and is wearing jeans on the bottom. Just a pair of old and faded jeans, but he is so fucking hot I can barely contain myself.

He laughs a little and I pull away, my hands still touching him, still caressing him. I slip a finger inside his waistband and he actually gasps.

"Do you like that?" I ask.

"You're trouble, Rook." He smiles and takes my hand and pushes it down farther and I feel the little hairs that run the length of his belly. I pull on one and he takes my mouth again. His hands are on my ass now, slipping inside the little boxer shorts and squeezing my cheeks.

A moan actually escapes my lips and the camera shutters are so loud I almost have to look at them.

I'd forgotten they were there to be honest.

Ronin won't tolerate the distraction, his hand dips between my cheeks and his finger tickles me between my legs.

My head drops back as I gasp and then he's holding my face again, his mouth taking me completely. I begin to rake my fingers through his hair when he abruptly spins me around so I'm facing forward, straight at the cameras.

"Do not look at them, Rook. Forget about them, OK?"

The throb between my legs is making it very hard to even open my eyes at this point, so I have no intention of looking at anyone, let alone the photographers. Ronin's fingers resume their undoing of the shirt buttons and I know this is the scary moment. Up until now it's just been a public makeout session. A heady one, for sure. But nothing obscene.

"Tell me what to do, Rook. You're in charge."

I don't even have to think about it. I turn my head up to him and he leans down in response, tilting his ear towards me. I breathe out, and I feel him shudder as it tickles him like he just tickled me, then whisper, as softly as I possibly can, "*Go.*"

"I'm going to bare you to them, are you sure?"

"Go," I repeat.

I expect him to rip the clothing off me in a rush, but he doesn't. Two fingers grasp the collar of the shirt and tug it slowly, fractionally, down one shoulder. He leans down and nibbles my neck and I almost lose it right there. My clit is throbbing, pulsating to the beat of my racing heart.

I reach my arms up and back so I'm grasping the back of his head. This must be magic for the photographers because they go wild at this move. I tip my head back so far, I'm almost looking at Ronin upside down. He claims my mouth and pulls one arm down and slips that half of the shirt off. I pull my arm out, exposing my breast. His fingers are instantly there, flicking my nipple and then pinching it, making me whimper.

I bite his lip in response and he growls, forcing my

other arm down.

The shirt slips all the way off and drifts to the floor.

He claims my wrists and brings them back over his head and I respond by pushing my ass into him. He is so hard.

I wiggle against it and then one hand is caressing my breast while the other travels down my belly, slips inside my boy shorts and goes right between my legs where the throbbing is so profound I think he might actually be able to feel the pulsations against his wet fingertip.

He flicks my clit and pushes his finger inside me and a feeling I have never felt before begins to build in me.

The moan escapes my mouth and it is *loud*, but all I can think about is Ronin's fingers as they play with me and then that feeling is there, like a wave getting ready to break on the beach, rushing forward, building and building, just beginning to crest and—

"Stop!"

What?

Who the fuck said stop?

"Ronin, what the hell are you doing? Rook, this is over now." Elise drapes a white robe over my shoulders and escorts me away from the crowd of people. Everyone stares at me, their eyes wide and their mouths gaping open as I pass.

"What? What happened? I don't understand!"

"He's got you way too worked up, Rook, this is not how we typically operate."

"I don't get it, isn't that his job? To work me up so you guys get good pictures?"

She opens my studio apartment door and pushes me inside but doesn't follow.

"He's supposed to make it feel real, not bring you to orgasm in front of a dozen people!"

And then she slams my door and leaves.

And I'm standing mostly naked in my new apartment, very pissed off that my clit is still throbbing like crazy and Ronin's magic fingers are outside and he is at this very moment—I know because I'm peeking out the front window—being bitched out by his sister.

Chapter Thirty-One

Ronin

"What the fuck, Ronin?"

Elise is so angry she's stabbing me in the chest with little staccato pokes of her finger. Her nails are long and pointy, so this does not feel pleasant. I glance over at Rook's window and find her face and grin.

"Ronin, stop smiling at her! I assured her this wouldn't happen and you made me a liar."

"She told me to go, Elise. Why would I stop? She was enjoying herself."

She pulls me along until we are back inside the studio. I'm assuming so Rook cannot see us.

"Ronin, this girl is fragile, do you understand? Much too fragile to make a rational decision about what is and is not appropriate on her first serious modeling job. You are the professional here and you know better!"

"Yeah, but this one's kinda like my girlfriend."

"All the more reason to protect her from this, you stupid piece of shit! Why do you think Antoine has me doing make-up and hair?"

I sigh and scrub my hands across my face. She's right. What the hell was I thinking? "OK, I get it. It's just that she drives me crazy and she said *go*, so..." I have no excuse. "Sorry, I lost control." I look down at Elise and nod. "I won't let it happen again, OK? I promise."

Elise and I both stop talking as the photographers come back inside. Roger laughs as he passes. "Way to go, Flynn. That was quite a show. This campaign is in the bag."

When I look back to Elise she's shaking her head. "You better make this right, Ronin. She's all worked up with the passion right now, but once she realizes these pictures are going out to clients, she's gonna be pissed."

I walk over to the terrace window and peek through at her window. Her face is gone now and I wonder what she's thinking. "Will you go talk to her?"

"No way. That's your job. You did this, now you fix it."

She looks at me for several seconds, her head tilting. I know this look, it says she's got an idea. "What?"

"Antoine and I have tickets for a fundraiser at the zoo, but he's meeting with Spence and the STURGIS team tonight."

"Oh, that sucks. Sorry, sis."

"Take Rook instead."

I shoot her a dirty look. "Now you want me to take her out, but yesterday you were threatening my manhood if I got anywhere near her? What's the deal?"

"Spencer is here and he's got that look, Ronin. Don't let him swoop in because you know he'll try. Let her choose a dress from the closet and take her to the fundraiser. I have a feeling she'll enjoy herself. Oh, and write a check on your way out. A big one."

And then she pats my cheek a few times and walks

off.

A night at the zoo. For a fundraiser. I'm not sure about this. It sounds like I have to wear a tux. I think about this for a second, then wander into the closet. It also means I could pick Rook out a nice sexy dress. I make my way over to the evening gowns and start looking for something red, long in length, and plunging at the neckline. I grab the dress and some shoes that look like her size, and then put it in a garment bag and hang it on the rack with Rook's name tag.

I hope she likes it.

Next on the list is the girly stuff, so I head over to the salon and talk Josie into making Rook up for the occasion. She agrees if I tip her generously, which I do because I figure if Rook has to worry about hair and make-up she'll probably say no.

Walking across the terrace makes me nervous for some reason. This girl who has not even been in my life for one week completely dominates all my thoughts. I mean, she's on my mind every second of the day. Even when Clare and I were fighting this morning, the only thing on my mind was how Rook was going to perceive that manic display of insanity from Clare.

I told Antoine I'm done with that girl. If Clare wants to jump off the ledge, fuck—there's nothing more I can do. I cut her loose and that's the end of it. Antoine was not happy, but whatever. He's never been able to control Clare and I've only ever had a tenuous hold on her at best. But all of that has left the building these days.

I can only hope that Rook doesn't read too much into it.

I stand at her door and knock, again feeling just a little bit off balance from all the recent changes. Rook answers in a pair of shorts and a halter top. My eyes take her in, from her perky nipples standing at attention, to her long legs, to her bare feet.

Which have painted pink toenails and are fidgeting around like she's Gidget talking on the phone or something.

I take a deep breath.

"Hey," she says, seductively leaning against the door jamb, jutting her hip off to the side and twirling her long raven-black hair around a finger. All she needs is some gum and she'd be the Gidget of my dreams.

"Hey," I say back, like an idiot. "Uh, I was wondering if you'd like to go to the zoo with me tonight?"

That sounded lame.

She coughs down a laugh. "The zoo?"

"Yeah, it's a fundraiser. Antoine and Elise were gonna go, but they have to work tonight. So she gave me their tickets."

"What are we raising funds for?"

"I have no idea." *Fuck, all I want to do is take you upstairs and throw you on my bed and hold you down while I make you scream my name.* I hope to fucking God I did not just say that out loud.

She doesn't laugh or squirm, so I guess I'm safe. "Is it fancy?"

"Yes, very. But I have a dress for you and Josie said she'll do your hair and make-up. What do you say?"

"You picked my dress?"

Oh, shit. I probably fucked up with that move. "Uh, well, you can pick something else if you want, but it's sexy as hell." I waggle my eyebrows at her and grin like an idiot, hoping to defuse that blunder.

"Does it make me look like Gidget?"

"No," I say too quickly. "Not at all."

"Well, in that case, I'll go. What do I have to do?"

I take her hand and tug her out the door. "I'll take care of everything, just relax and I'll meet you outside the dressing room at seven."

I drop her off with Josie and get the hell out of there before she can change her mind or ask me anything else about fruit baskets and vacant bedrooms on the lower floors of the building, then take the stairs up to my apartment three at time and go searching for my tux.

Chapter Thirty-Two

Josie does my hair in an up-do. It doesn't take long, all she has to do is brush it out and pin it up, swooping it over to one side, while the top and back are sufficiently poofed up to give it some height. When she shows me in the mirror I let out a small gasp. Even without the make-up and dress, I already look better than ever before. The hair is sleek, not messy and half falling out like most up-dos end up, but shiny and pulled tight.

Josie smiles when I look over at her. "That's how fashion models do the up-do, Rook. Don't ever let them give you those wispy tendrils again!"

As if I ever had wispy tendrils to bag on. "Thank you, it's perfect."

"Now, for make-up, you don't need much. Some foundation and bronzer, then red lips. Ronin said the dress was red, so you must have lips to match. I'll put a sealer coat over it, so it will last."

She does it just like she said and then sets me off to find my clothes in the dressing room. It's past six now, so the whole place is quiet. I find my bag and take it over to the upholstered benches in the middle of the outer dressing area where all the naked girls were earlier. This time I get shoes, and I'm relieved because my ripped-up Converse would never do for the absolutely stunning red creation I pull out of the bag.

Maybe Ronin is a control freak, but he has good taste in dresses. I hold it up to my body and it falls to the floor like it was made specifically for me. I guess it was, really, since I'm a standard model size and all these clothes are made for people who have a shape and height like mine.

It's strapless and has two slits that go all the way up to my mid-thigh on each side. The neckline is not low enough so my girls are hanging out if I move and the fabric is incredibly soft. I have no clue what it's made of, but it's soft. The bodice is trimmed in a few clear sparkles, just enough to make it twinkle in the lights, but not enough to make me look like a disco ball. After helping myself to some new panties from the underwear drawer, I wiggle into it and reach around to draw up the zipper. I only make it halfway, but I'm sure Ronin won't mind finishing that off for me.

I chuckle when I think about him. Gah, this man! I'm not sure what to do with him. He made me feel incredible today. Seriously, I've never had an orgasm. Sex was not something I enjoyed in the past, but after experiencing what he can do to me, I'm hoping that is about to change.

When I slip my feet in the shoes and realize they are not only my size, but comfortable to boot, I almost give in to his controlling ways. He really does know what he's doing. Is it so bad to trust someone to take care of you?

"Rook?"

"Come in," I yell back.

He walks in and I about have a heart attack. He's

wearing a tux. "Oh, my," we say at the same time. And then we both burst out laughing.

"I feel like a grown-up," he says, looking down at himself.

"Mr. Flynn, you definitely look like a grown up." His tux is the kind that rock stars wear to those award ceremonies—black on black with slim-fit trousers. He walks straight over to me without hesitation and wraps his hands around my hips. His touch releases a fire that travels all through my body.

"Do you need a hand with the zipper, Gidge?" he asks, leaning down into my ear.

I want to say *yeah, but not the way you think*. I want him unzipping me right now. I want him to lift me up, slam me against the dressing room wall, and take me right here. Fuck this dress, this fundraiser, and everything else!

"Yes, please," is what really comes out.

Darn stupid inhibitions.

He turns me around, his hands trailing around my waist, and then his fingertips dance along my bare back for a moment before he gently lifts the zipper. I twist a bit at his touch and let out a gasp when he leans in to kiss the back of my neck.

"Did I tickle you?" he asks, leaning in closer as I turn back to face him. His breath teases my throat and then his lips travel up and flutter against the soft skin under my ear.

"No, you excite me, Larue. You make all my Gidget parts tingle." I giggle as his tongue continues to tease my throat and then I have to shake my whole head to dampen down the shudder of pleasure that runs through my body.

"You're gonna make me want to forget all about this night out if you're not careful. And then I'll have Elise mad at me for wasting the tickets and Josie mad at me for wasting the beautiful job she did on your hair and makeup. Now, hold still."

Something cold slides against my chest and Ronin's hands clasp together a piece of jewelry around my neck. I look down and bite my lip at the gemstones as they sparkle in the overhead lights of the dressing room.

He turns me around and steps back, hands never leaving my body. "I have no words for you, Rook Walsh."

"Try," I whisper back as I stare hungrily into his eyes.

He brings his palms to my face and tilts my chin. "I could describe what you look like, but that's not what I see. You are so much more than a body inside a dress, Rook. You fit me. When I saw you crouching in that stairwell last week I felt like I knew you. You stopped me dead in my tracks, you wiped my mind. And I reached out to touch you that day because I couldn't resist. I needed to do it and I plan on touching you all night, on the way there in the car, through dinner, as we walk around the zoo and do whatever the hell it is they do at a nighttime fundraiser, and all the way home."

"And then?" I prod.

He lets out a soft laugh. "Oh, Miss Walsh, I plan on doing many more things to you tonight, but most of all, when I finally get you back to my apartment and into my bed, I plan on making you whimper into my neck, begging me to make you come."

Whoa! I think I need a new pair of panties. I breathe in deeply and wait for him to laugh or do something to break the mood.

But he doesn't.

He stares at me and then dips down to my neck again to whisper in my ear. "I'd crush your mouth with kisses right now if I thought I could get away with smearing your lipstick."

And then we do laugh. I take another deep breath and he offers me his arm. I grab hold of that arm like I never want to let go. We take the elevator down instead of the stairs and when we exit the garage, there's a town-car waiting to take us to the zoo.

A long breath escapes as the driver holds the door open for us. I get in and scoot across the butter-soft leather seat, then Ronin joins me and the door closes with a soft whoosh.

"What?" he asks.

"Just wow." I look over at him and laugh a little. "I mean, I've never..." The sentence just drops off because I seriously have no words for how I feel right now. "I've never been on a date like this." I look over at him and he's got a crooked grin on his face.

"Then you're long overdue, Gidget."

The car pulls out of the parking garage and I watch the street outside as Ronin puts his arm around my shoulders and pulls me a little closer to him. "How far away is the zoo?"

"Not far, just over in City Park."

"So have you lived here in Denver your whole life?"

"Yeah, Five Points, born and bred." He shrugs, like he's apologizing.

"Is that a good thing? Or not? You seem to be leaving something unsaid."

"It's not Park Hill, let's just leave it at that. Elise and I grew up in a house just down the street from our building. It was a total shit hole."

"Oh. Does it bother you to be in the same neighborhood?"

"No. I can't explain it, but even though there's a lot of nasty shit that happens on our side of town, it's home for me. And where we are, things are more quiet than in some places. I can see the draw of moving over to Cherry Creek or Park Hill or Highland's Ranch, but I'm not ashamed of where I started. You can't choose your parents." He shrugs.

I internalize this for a few moments. "You could be talking about me."

His eyes come back to me and he waits a few seconds before speaking. "I wasn't though. I have no idea how you grew up."

I swallow down the bad memories. "Pretty much the same as you, except for the French knight in shining armor thing. I never got one of those."

"*Vous avez tort, mon amour. Je suis juste ici.*"

"What's that mean?"

He leans in and nuzzles my ear. "It means the bad stuff is over now, Gidget, and the good is just about to start." My whole body flushes and he laughs in my neck as the car stops. "We're here. When's the last time you were at a zoo?"

"Never," I admit.

He pulls back as the driver gets out to open our door. "That's criminal! How can a child grow up in America and never go to the zoo?"

I shrug. "My childhood was a long string of foster homes and crack houses." I watch his eyes as the door opens from the outside. "Sometimes," I continue, "I had both at the same time. The Chicago foster care system is not ideal."

He's crushed as the words sink in. His hand reaches over and grabs mine off my lap and he shakes his head. "I had no idea, Rook. Maybe we shouldn't go in?"

"Why?" I ask, startled, my heart racing in my chest.

"Because this fundraiser is for foster care kids. I didn't

know, I swear. If it's not something you want to think about I'll take you somewhere else. Anywhere you want."

He raises his hand to brush against my cheek and for a moment I lose control. A little wave of hurt and sadness sweeps over me and I feel the pool of tears that threaten my perfect night. But I swallow it down. "No," I say, shaking my head. "No way. I'm not responsible for where I came from. I didn't choose that life, I chose this one. This night isn't about me, it's about them," I say, pointing to the zoo entrance. "I want to go in." He hesitates, but I nod and say it again. "I swear, I want to go in. Come on, let's go."

We get out of the car and walk towards the entrance where Ronin hands our tickets to the ushers. They point us down a pathway that veers off to the right and then hand us a program.

"Want to walk around a little?" Ronin asks. "We have about twenty minutes."

"Yes, please. What's close by?"

Ronin studies the map on the back of the program and leads us past the event center. "Elephants!" he says with a laugh. "Once, Antoine took Elise and me to India for some big fashion thing. We'd just met the guy, we'd known him for like three months I guess. And he sprang this trip on us and even though I thought Antoine was a total dick because he refused to speak English to me, that trip to India was awesome because I got to ride an elephant. Of course," he says, looking sideways at me, "I tried to pretend I was unimpressed with the whole thing. Kids, right? They never appreciate anything."

"Wow. India. I can't even imagine how cool that would be."

"Well, you know, they got their problems, the shit's the same the world over. Some places are nicer than others. But Antoine was photographing some important people so we got special treatment. It was cool."

We stop in front of the elephant enclosure and stare at nothing. There are no elephants in sight. "Oh, look, you have to go inside," he says.

I'm not sure I want to go in the pachyderm house in this dress, but Ronin pulls me so I'm forced to follow. Inside there is a table set up and two zoo workers are chatting with the event visitors about sponsoring an elephant. The elephants just munch on hay and give us all dirty looks.

Ronin grabs some literature as we shuffle though with the other guests, then find ourselves outside where the hint of rain becomes a light drizzle. We get caught up in the wave that brings us back to the event center, get escorted to our table, and take our seats as the presentations start.

I've never been to a charity anything, let alone some big production put on to squeeze money out of the pockets of Denver's rich and famous. There are quite a few presenters and Ronin actually knows a few people who appear on stage.

Which is weird. Because I just don't see him as the rich and snooty type, but I guess Chaput Studios is a major player in this town. There are a few kids who give their touching stories and a few older kids, the same age as me probably, who talk about the great families they had in foster care.

After the presentations and plea for money, dinner is served. Ronin chats easily with the other couples at our table between bites of prime rib. They are all friends of Elise and Antoine's and they don't seem at all disappointed that Ronin and I had to step in and take their place for the evening. They ask us a ton of questions about pretty much everything. It's funny how once you get older, questions that normally seem rude become standard. Like, *So when's the wedding?*

I almost snort some ice out of my nose at this one.

Ronin doesn't even flinch, he just promises to send the couple an invitation once we nail it down.

I smile into my water glass at that.

The night just flies by and before I know it Ronin is writing a check and then we're huddling underneath a large black umbrella as we make our way back to the parking lot in the pouring rain.

We both scoot into the back into the car and breathe a sigh of relief.

"Was it fun, Gidge?" Ronin asks me as he brings my legs up over his lap, then slips my shoes off my aching feet and starts to rub them.

"Yes, it was fun… oh, God, that feels good!"

"I told you I was gonna touch you all the way home."

And all during the night, which he did. I can barely recall a second when his hand was not on me in some way. If it wasn't draped over the back of my chair, gently teasing the back of my neck, it was on my knee, squeezing lightly as the other couples did their best to embarrass us with questions about babies.

But the really interesting thing about all this touching is how I feel about it. A few days ago I might have seen it as possessive, but tonight it felt like affection. Maybe that means I'm getting over some of the bad things that happened to me in Chicago?

I hope so. Because I like Ronin Flynn for sure now.

"What're you thinking about?" Ronin asks me as the town car makes its way through the traffic in the parking lot.

"Just kinda reevaluating my thoughts on certain

things." I shoot him a sideways glance. "About you mostly."

"Yeah? Is that good or bad?'

"Good, I think. I mean, I'm still a bit of a mess personally. But maybe I was wrong about you? Maybe you are a good guy?"

"Did you really think I was a bad guy?" he says, his brow in a furrow.

"No. Yes. Well," I sigh. "I'm probably not the best judge right now, Ronin. I'm tainted by past experiences, so I'm not sure I can tell the difference anymore."

"Well, let me ask you this, have I ever hurt you?"

"No."

"Did the last guy hurt you?"

I look away and let the question hang there as I take a deep breath. "Very badly," I finally manage.

"So now you doubt your decisions? About choosing the right guy to date?"

"Sorta."

He waits because we both know that's not an answer.

"I just never want to get in that situation again. I never want to be controlled like that. What I do want," I say, looking him in the eye now, "is to be myself and not get mowed down by a boyfriend's personality, or dreams, or needs. I want to make my own money so I never have to depend on a guy again. Does that make any sense?" He nods, slowly. His hands are still massaging my feet and I lean my head sideways on the back of the seat and try to relax as I listen to the rain pound the roof of the car.

"I get it, Rook. I have the same problem, except in reverse."

I open my eyes and look at him. "What do you mean?"

"Well, I have this rule that I won't date a model,

right? I mean, I break it all the time," he laughs a little, "obviously. But the part I won't break is where these encounters will end up. I want a normal life with a normal family. I don't want to bring kids up in Antoine's studio. I don't want my wife taking her clothes off so I can touch her in front of the camera. I want *boring.* I want kids in Catholic school and a minivan filled with car seats. And I have no idea how long this thing with Antoine's studio will last, but I'm pretty sure that I'd rather die than be the father of a teenage girl who runs the models at an erotic art photography studio."

I smile a little at that thought. He's right. That's a disaster waiting to happen.

The car pulls into the studio parking garage and Ronin slips my shoes back on. We wait for the driver in silence, then make our way to the elevator and head on upstairs.

"So where's that leave us?" Ronin asks.

I shrug. "I dunno," I say honestly. I have never fantasized about getting married and having children, not even as a child, because I have no good memories of that kind of life. But this seems to be a big deal to Ronin and I don't want to ruin our perfect night, so I follow up my shrug with something evasive. "I guess we'll just have to wait and see what happens."

Chapter Thirty-Three

Ronin

When the elevator doors open Rook and I are bombarded with studio lights and general chaos. Elise is barking orders at technicians and Antoine spies us from across the room and is already yelling out in French as he crosses the distance.

"What's going on?" Rook asks me.

"Rain shoot," I say, picking up every third word coming out of Antoine's mouth due to the scraping of a ladder across the floor. I feel Rook tense at the screeching noise. "We have to get a shot in the rain for TRAGIC." I should've anticipated this, really. But I stopped thinking about work hours ago.

I put my hand up as Antoine approaches, but I know it's useless. There's no getting out of it, we have to shoot tonight. Now. "Go with Elise, she'll get you ready."

"Wait." She grabs a hold of my arm. "We have to work *right now*?"

"Yeah, sounds like fun, huh?"

She rolls her eyes at me.

"Rook, nine times out of ten, being a model sucks. Better get used to it if this is the life you want." I push her towards Elise and sigh. I know it's a dig at her declaration of independence, but I can't help it. The last thing I want is this girl half naked in the cold rain at night. But it's in the contract that we get a rain shot, so it must be done.

Elise whisks Rook off to the salon to wash her makeup off and take her hair down. I take the stairs to my apartment three at a time and head straight for my closet.

I hang up the tux and try not to let the disappointment wash over me as I trade my expensive clothes for an old pair of jeans and a white t-shirt. Rook will be wearing the exact same thing, except she'll have a nice black bra on so that when she's soaking wet it will show through the fabric for everyone to see.

And that just pisses me off. Elise was right, I should be protecting her from this life, not encouraging her to give Antoine what he wants.

I take a few deep breaths to dampen down the anger and then pull on a pair of boots and head back downstairs. Antoine is waiting for me, still barking orders, but clearly waiting for me because he's blocking the stairs. He sends the technician off and turns as I try to push past him.

"Ronin, wait."

I shake my head. "Tonight, Antoine?"

"It might not rain again."

"It's called a fucking shower. We could just do it inside, in the warm fucking shower room."

"I want city lights," he says, like this explains everything.

"So fucking what?"

"Her contract is with me and I decide what we shoot. If you're too attached to her, then I can get someone else to finish the job."

"You're funny tonight, ya know that?"

"The quicker we get started, the quicker we can be done. Go."

He pushes me and I pull back out of his reach just as Rook comes out of the dressing room. Just as I predicted, white t-shirt, faded jeans, and a nice black bra that everyone can see. I smile at her because she looks worried.

"Hey," I say, accepting an umbrella from one of the techs standing by the terrace door. I open it and we walk outside together. The rain is pelting down with such force against the umbrella I have a hard time hearing what she's saying.

"What?"

"This sucks," she screams in my ear.

"Yeah," I agree, squeezing her arm a little.

"And I'm freezing!"

"It just gets worse, Gidget. So better to just put on the game-face and push on, because the sooner fuckwad Antoine gets his piece-of-shit pictures, the sooner we can go to bed."

She looks up at me. "We?"

I smile and let the anger wash off me, but I let that question hang there. It's hard to predict how this will turn out. Maybe good, maybe not.

We have a special platform that we do the city light shots on. It's raised up about six feet off the terrace floor and basically it's just a slab of concrete that has a railing, so it looks like you're on a terrace, but it gives Antoine lots of different ways to approach the photo. Tonight we have a tarp set up to protect everyone except Rook and me from the rain, and all the exterior lights are on. We have a mock street lamp and spotlights that are mounted on the ground. We slip under the tarp and I hand the umbrella off to someone who looks like he's about to pass out from fatigue. It's after two in the morning, so I can't blame him, I feel the same way.

"OK, Rook, let's just get this done as quick as possible. We go out in the rain, they adjust the lights, we make out, wiggle around a little, start undressing each other, I get you down to the bra and panties, end of shoot. Got it?" She starts shivering the minute I say the word undressing, and by the time I'm done talking her teeth are chattering.

"I'm f-f-fre-eeeezing," she repeats, her arms all drawn up against her body.

I hug her close and she melts into my chest. "I know. As soon as we're done I'll warm you back up, OK?"

She nods, but the chattering continues.

"OK, let's go." I pull her out into the rain with me and the shit is coming down so hard it actually stings my skin. I look over at Rook as I get into position and she's frantically trying to straighten out her wet hair. Elise appears in a rain slicker and begins adjusting her hair, leaning in to tell her encouraging things as she does it.

When Elise leaves I lean against the fake light pole and pull Rook into me again. She's very willing and this makes me smile. "Put your arms around me, Gidge. You'll get warmer, and besides, mauling my body is part of the job assignment tonight. This job has awesome benefits, doesn't it?"

She laughs and wraps her arms around my waist. Antoine is already shooting, so I slip my hands inside the edge of her t-shirt. It's plastered against her body already, we are fully soaked.

Antoine barks orders at the techs to adjust the lighting, but I tune them all out and concentrate on Rook.

I lean down into her ear as her body trembles with cold against me. "Forget them. Forget the rain. Forget the job. Look at me."

She looks up.

"It's just us. Pretend we're in the warm car, all dressed, and we can't wait to get home so we can rip each other's clothes off."

"You have mind-reading powers, don't you?"

"What?" I laugh.

She winks at me. "You were reading my mind back there in the car, weren't you?"

I lean down and kiss her, just a soft flutter kiss to let her know I'm interested in playing. "You're on to me, huh?"

"I am," she coos back. "But do you know what I was thinking *after* I fantasized about ripping off your clothes?"

I nod.

"Tell me."

"You were thinking that maybe I'd take my hands and slip them inside your shirt, like this." My fingers travel up her ribcage, a light drag that makes her gasp and hold in a giggle, and then I push against her breast. "And I was thinking about how I wasn't allowed to kiss you all night because of your lipstick. But now, it's all gone."

"Mmmmhhhmmm," she moans as I take my kisses to her neck.

"So now, I can ravish your mouth properly." I withdraw my hand from under her shirt and I absently log Antoine complaining that he wants me to take the damn shirt off, not lose focus, but I grasp Rook's face with both hands, lift her up to me, so all her attention is on my face and nothing else. And then I crush her lips with my kiss. The heat of her mouth and the twirl of her tongue against mine makes me hard in an instant. I grind against her a little and she moans back at me, that little thrum of her voice against my palm driving me crazy.

I rip my own shirt off in one fluid motion. Antoine goes crazy with this move, and not in a good way—he likes the girls to play with that a little, but fuck him. Rook's hands start in on my chest, tracing a stream of water that is racing down my body. Her fingertip starts at my shoulder and then falls down, the water bouncing off it, splattering a little, as she traces over my muscle, then continues as the tiny river is lost in the waistband of my pants.

Her finger slips in, just a tiny fraction, just enough to drive me up a fucking wall with desire. I feel her laugh a little and I pull back.

"You think you're in control here, Gidge?"

She nods, blushing.

I begin lifting her shirt away from her body, it's so wet now, it's plastered to her skin. I rub it against her belly as I lift and she moans, making me rush a little, showing her bra. It's a demi, so it dips very low, almost exposing her nipples. The shirt comes off a few seconds later and I can hear Antoine telling me what to do, but I dismiss him.

I know exactly what I'm doing. I take her whole breast in my hand and squeeze until she whimpers, then drop my mouth to her nipple and drag the fabric down with my teeth. She fists my hair and I lift her up until her legs wrap around my waist. I turn and push her against the light pole, and she is panting into my ear as I suck.

"Pants! Ronin! We're all cold here!" Antoine barks.

I shift Rook until I have her weight distributed against my hip, just the one hand holding her up, then lift my other hand towards Antoine.

And flip him off.

And then I gather Rook against me, pushing the heat between her legs into my thick hardness, walk off the set, down the stairs, and over to her apartment. I crash her against the outside wall as I punch in the codes and whisk her inside. My foot comes out and kicks the door closed, and then I carry her down the short hallway and throw her down on the bed.

"If you want me to stop, please," I beg, "say it now."

She licks her lips as I stare down her with hungry eyes, and then whispers, "I don't want you to stop, Ronin. I don't want to take it slow or change direction. I just want you to go. *Please*, I'm fucking dying here, just go!"

Chapter Thirty-Four

He laughs at my plea, but shit! I've never had an orgasm and right now I'm on the edge. It's like I can feel that fucker ready to explode, I need the teeniest bit of pressure in just the right spot and I will gush all over him.

All the caveman shit from outside is gone now and he watches my face as he works on the front clasp of my bra. My breasts fall out as he unfastens it, and then I sit up and wiggle my arms out and he tosses it across the room.

"Lie down," he commands.

I do.

His hands go to my jeans and after some unbuttoning, he grabs them by the waist and pulls them down so fast they end up inside out because they are wet and plastered to my legs. His fingers go to my panties and he tugs a little until I lift my hips. He slides them down my legs and drops them to the floor.

I lie still, completely naked, as his eyes take me in. "Your turn," I say in a throaty whisper.

His fingers unbutton his jeans and unzip the fly and

then he steps out of them and his boxers in one movement. He's well-built and I try not to stare, but I don't entirely succeed. When I look up at his face, he's smiling.

"What?"

"You, Gidget. You're blushing."

"I'm not very experienced," I admit. "I'm not a virgin, but it was all pretty boring and I've never—"

He waits a few seconds and then prods me on as he lies down next to me. "You've never what?"

His hands caress my stomach and I relax against the pillows. My wet clothes have made everything damp on the bed, but I do not care. "I've never had an orgasm."

I expect him to laugh or make a joke, but he doesn't. He just leans over my body, pressing himself up to me, his erection grinding against my hip. I am desperate to get him inside me, but he's slow now. "I might not be able to make many guarantees in this world, Rook," he says as his hand travels down and traces the crease between my legs. "But I will say with one hundred percent certainty that you will come tonight."

He leans down to my face as his fingers probe into my entrance and teases my lips with a nibble as he pushes one finger inside me, and then uses his thumb to gently caress my clit. I squirm as his kiss becomes bruising, my whole body on fire with the desire I have.

"Oh, God, Ronin. Please, I am so close." My hands reach down and grab his shaft, pumping him, making him breathe heavy and moan out my name. That talented finger of his flicks against me in just the right way and the agonizing throb that has been building for the last week suddenly explodes. I shove my face into his neck and bite his ear, which only makes him work my clit harder and send a wave of wetness between my legs.

He lets me pant there in the crook of his neck as the tiny flutter waves flow through me for a few more minutes, and then he lies back and pulls me on top of him, his erection peeking out from between my legs. "You can be on top, Gidget. Do you like it on top?"

"I have no idea," I admit again.

"I think you will. Lift up for a second."

I lift my hips and he slides his cock back and forth across my slit, murmuring approval as he enjoys the wetness he created with his fingers. And then I feel the pressure. His hands have a hold of my hips now and he urges me to push down on him and I feel him stretch me as he pushes up.

"Fuck, Rook, I can't believe how good you feel." Ronin stares up with me, his eyes barely open as I lift up and then push down one more time. I shift a little as I come down, my clit rubbing up against the base of his shaft, and holy fucking shit, that feels good. I do it again and this time I exert a little more force as I come down, making Ronin growl out a few unintelligible words.

His hands thrust me up and then slam me down, and everything I just experienced is magnified, I can feel the pressure building inside me again. I lift up, getting into his faster rhythm, and we slam together harder and harder with each movement and just when I think I'm going to come again, he slows it down, and instead of the thrusting, he draws me down onto his chest and grabs my ass with both hands, sliding me, sliding my clit, back and forth across his body. We come together this time, a collective of pleasure and panting, as his mouth crashes against mine once more, our tongues still desperate for each other.

When the shock waves subside I burrow my head into his neck again, then collapse against his chest. He turns me over so I'm on my side and then slips his arm under me, pulling my ass up against his stomach. "It was better than the fantasy, Rook. I'd just like you to know that."

I lie there for a few seconds, so happy I can hardly stand it. So satisfied with his body pressed up against me, his breath lingering on my neck as he relaxes. And I fall asleep with a man I might love for real, for the first time ever.

Chapter Thirty-Five

A loud knock jolts me out of my sleep and I turn so fast, I fall out of bed.

I'm naked.

And when I look around in a half-asleep daze, I also realize I'm alone. I'm pretty sure Ronin was here when I fell asleep.

The knocking comes again and I wrap the sheet around me and hustle my ass down the hallway to the door. I can see Elise's face peeking through the window so I relax a little.

"Jesus," she says. "Heavy sleeper or what?" Her hands are clasping a clipboard piled with papers.

I can barely see her though the gunk in my eyes, so I don't answer, but that should be her second clue that yes, indeed, I am a heavy sleeper.

"Why are you here?" I manage to croak out.

"Time to work."

"What time is it?" I ask, confused. I look around, still trying to put things together.

"Seven-thirty."

"What the hell? I just went to bed a few hours ago, Elise! You guys had me out in the freaking rain in the middle of the night!"

"Yeah, well, today we need to make you look like shit for this shoot, so what better way to look like shit than to feel like shit? Besides, Ronin is gone for the day and Antoine wants to shoot you with Billy for this."

"Billy! But—"

"Hey, don't push it right now, Rook, you guys pissed him off last night pretty bad. He needs some slutty shots and he wants someone to take care of you in the shoot, so that's Billy for today."

"Yeah, because that went so well last time," I mutter.

"That was a misunderstanding, Billy is just fine. He's worked for us for almost two years so relax. Don't shower, just put some clothes on and come right to make-up."

She turns on her heel and some of her papers flutter off the clipboard and float down at my feet. I reach down, still slightly dazed from sleep, and go to hand them back to her when I realize what I'm holding.

It's a contact sheet filled with pictures. Pictures of Ronin and me from yesterday.

The view in each one is from below, like whoever took this shot was on the ground looking up at us. Front and center is Ronin's hand inside my boxer shorts and there is no way to miss the fact that his fingers are definitely between my legs. The other hand gropes my breast with a force that appears to be bruising. My head is tilted back, my mouth open in what I can only imagine was a groan of pleasure, but it's Ronin's face that stops me cold.

He's looking straight at the camera. His electric blue

eyes blazing like a predator, his brows furrowed together, and his lips in a snarl. He looks like an animal ready to take down a kill. And I get it, it's theatrics for the sake of art. Or whatever. But he made such a big deal about not looking at the camera, and here he is, staring directly into it?

It feels like a betrayal.

"What the fuck is this?" I ask Elise.

She draws in a deep breath and takes the photo back. "That is the winning image, Rook. They loved it. Congratulations, you're about to be famous."

And then she turns around and walks off, leaving me standing in the doorway.

Is this what I signed up for? Of all the images they got of us yesterday, that was the one they have to use? Where the hell did Ronin go? That's really not cool. And slutty shots? I don't even want to know what that means.

"Hurry up!" Elise calls out as I stand there thinking.

I slam the door and go put on some clothes, brush my teeth real fast, slip on my ratty old Converse, and head over to make-up.

Why I am sent there I have no idea because when Josie turns me around to look at myself, I look like shit. Just like Elise wanted. I have raccoon eyes from the smeared eye shadow, my lipstick is splotchy, and she has applied some kind of make-up in just the right way to make my face look hollowed out.

I am a crack whore.

I am my mother.

In that instant I see her. The same eyes, the same raven-black hair, the same look of impending death.

I look over at Elise, who is impatient to get me in the dressing room, and shake my head.

"Yes, we need this shoot and we need to get it done

quick."

"Why? Why is it such a rush?"

She ignores me as we walk quickly into the dressing room. Everything about this day is wrong.

My clothes aren't in a bag, they are splayed out on one of the benches in the middle of the dressing room. It's only then that I realize there are no other girls around. "Elise, what's going on? Where is everyone?"

"We have meetings with the STURGIS people, the suits are here again, they're nailing down the specifics of the contract and Antoine is not happy, so please, just do what you're told and you'll be done fast and you can have the rest of the day off. Now put those clothes on and meet us down on the third floor."

Again, she walks out.

I look over the clothes and almost laugh. The shirt is dirty and torn, the jeans are the same, and the underwear—yes, I actually have underwear this time—is black. It comes with a demi bra, like the one I had on last night, and some boy shorts. I put the underwear on and then the clothes. The rip on the shirt goes right between my tits so the black bra is visible.

When I turn to look at myself in the mirror, I am a homeless crack whore.

I swallow down the bad feeling I'm getting about this day, slip my feet back into my sneakers, and walk down the stairs to the third floor.

Billy is waiting for me, checking his phone for a text or something. He looks up after his fingers finish their swiping, and smiles. "You look great!"

I'm not sure if he means I look great for this part I'm playing today or if that was a total joke, so I just say nothing.

"Oh, calm down, Rook. It's a simple shoot, no nudity

or nothing, Antoine said. Although I'm disappointed at that, to be honest. You are very hot. So I'm just supposed to tell you what to do. Antoine thinks it's weird if he tells you himself, so I'm playing moderator today, I guess. To keep Ronin at bay once he finds out we did this while he was busy with Clare."

"With Clare?" I ask, my heart beating fast.

"Yeah, he's down in the first floor apartment with her, sleeping it off or whatever."

Sleeping it off? What the fuck does that mean? "What first floor apartment?"

Billy opens a door and ushers me in with a wave of his hand. "One of the extra ones Ronin uses for his girls."

Holy shit. I feel like a total idiot.

"Rook!" Antoine barks. "Over here." He points to a makeshift bedroom and I do as I'm told because all I want right now is to finish this shoot and get the hell out of this place. He talks to Billy in some amalgam of French and English and then Billy is telling me what to do. He touches me, has his hands all over me, kisses me a few times even, but nothing about this shoot is anything like the ones I did with Ronin. Billy is all business, and I suppose that's good. I mean, if a strange guy is getting paid to maul you, I guess you'd want to keep it professional. But nothing can stop the horror of him stripping my clothes off, fondling my breasts, and then sitting me down in his lap, only in the underwear now, and placing my own hand between my legs as Antoine's camera clicks away.

And then it's over and I'm putting my clothes back on.

I have no idea what just happened, but I have never felt so fucking dirty in all my life.

Thankfully Billy takes my arm, chatting away

pleasantly like this is just another day, and walks me out to the hallway. I stop at the stairs and come to my senses.

"I'll see you later, huh?"

He just continues to climb the stairs and calls out, "Sure thing!"

I walk down the stairs slowly, talking myself into believing this is just a big misunderstanding. Ronin is not sleeping it off with Clare. He was with me last night. We didn't go to bed until three in the morning, at least. I woke up at seven thirty. When did he find the time to sleep with another girl?

I've never explored the other floors before but Ronin freely admitted to taking his fuck buddies into these rooms. When I get to the first floor I walk down the hallway and try every door. They are all open, they are all shabby, and they are all empty. When I get to the last door, the one near the back of the building right next to the fire exit, I see a keypad.

I punch in Ronin's code and the door clicks as it unlocks. I twist the handle and push it open quietly, listening for sounds of people. Nothing. I open it more and step inside, leaving the door open behind me.

And I hear a faint moan.

I force myself to walk into the living room. It's pretty clear someone is living here because this place is furnished, maybe not nicely, but adequately. And there are old food containers that have the Cookie's Diner logo on them.

And there are clothes strewn about the floor. Underwear.

I walk farther in, towards the sound that has since ceased, and stop at a bedroom door that is slightly ajar. I can see in and I can see a bed.

And on that bed is Clare and Ronin.

Sleeping it off.

My heart beats wildly as I back out of the apartment, quietly close the door behind me, and push open the emergency exit door to get away as fast as I can. I push through a second door and then I'm in the parking lot out back near the freight elevators.

There are a whole bunch of people loading motorcycles and I weave my way through them, bumping into people, almost knocking down a bike, just doing anything I can to get away from this place. I push past a big guy and he grabs me by the arm as I flee. I turn to fight him off when I realize it's Spencer.

"You OK, Rook?"

I just stare up into his blue eyes and shake my head. "No, I don't think I am." I look back at the building and shake my head again. "I'm not OK. I need to get out of here. I need to go." I pull away from his grip and start running down the alley but he catches me and pulls me back, almost yanking me back, until I slam into his chest.

"Hold on, what's going on? Did someone hurt you? Why are your clothes all ripped?"

I look down at my outfit and laugh. "Oh, fuck." He lets go of my arm and waits as I take a deep breath. "Sorry, no, no one hurt me. This was from the photoshoot, that's all, but I can't stay here right now. I just need to go someplace, anyplace. I just need to go."

He takes my arm again and guides me over to a big red Ford F-250 with the logo of his bike shop on it. "Here, take a seat, we'll go get some lunch. I wanted to talk to you about the contract anyway, before Antoine and Ronin exaggerate it all out of proportion. I want you to make up your own mind about whether or not it's a good fit, because frankly, I'm tired of hearing them tell me you're not interested when I think you might be. So sit tight, sister." He waits for me to settle in the passenger seat and then closes the door and heads over to his buddies who are unloading bikes from the back of a semi.

I watch the back door nervously, afraid I'm going to get caught. Where is this feeling coming from? I didn't do anything wrong!

But that's never stopped you from getting punished before, Rook.

I shake my head. Ronin is not Jon. Antoine is not Jon.

But they might not be the people I thought they were either.

Spencer comes back a few minutes later, climbs in, and turns to me. "Where should we go?"

"I don't care, I have no idea, just get me out of here. And not Cookie's, OK?"

He laughs. "I'd never take you to Cookie's, Blackbird. I'll take you to my favorite restaurant, how's that?"

I nod and chew on my nail as we drive away, my whole world spinning once again.

Chapter Thirty-Six

Spencer and I end up at a biker bar that is nowhere near Denver. And really, I asked for this, right? *Get me out of here* is code for *get me the fuck out of here*. I laugh at this as I eat my burger.

"What's funny?" Spence asks.

"Nothing, it's just… where the hell are we?"

He leans back in the booth and stretches his arms out to either side, obviously proud of himself. "My bar." He grins like an idiot now.

"This is your bar? Shit, dude, you're like loaded or what? You can't be any older than Ronin and you have all those bikes, some TV show people paying for a major deal with Antoine, and you own a bar?"

"You forgot Shrike Bikes showroom next door. Which is really where I want to take you so I can show you what this contract is all about."

"Why not just tell me? I mean, why's it such a secret?"

"Well, it sounds bad on paper."

I eye him suspiciously.

"But it's not, Rook. I swear, just let me show you because if Ronin and Antoine get to you first they'll blow it all up and make it sound dirty." He stops to lean forward and raise his eyebrows at me, but not in a joking way, he's almost pleading for me to understand. "It's not dirty. It's art. And it's a hell of a lot less exploitative than what you're doing for TRAGIC, I'll tell you that right now."

I pout at this, because today was just wrong. I had to wash my face in the bathroom when I got here and change into a spare biker shirt Spencer had in his truck because the whole crack-whore thing was not working for me. If this is what modeling for Antoine will be like most of the time, I'm not interested. "I'll keep an open mind, how's that?"

"Perfect, that's all I ask."

After we eat we walk over to his shop. It rained a little while we were inside, so water sloshes inside my worn-out Converse as we splash through some puddles. There are no sidewalks around here, just dirt. Spencer opens the door to the showroom for me and I'm a little taken aback by the beauty of it all. "Wow, you have some nice bikes, Spence. I had no idea."

"You're into the bike scene, Rook?" he asks, a bit surprised by my genuine interest.

I shrug and sigh at the same time because I was into the bike scene once, if only because of the person who got me interested in the first place.

"Which one do you like the best?" he asks me as I walk between the aisles of bikes lined up, headlight to headlight, facing each other. There must be like thirty or forty bikes in here.

"I like the retro ones, like this one right here," I say, tapping the glossy gas tank. "It looks like an old

Triumph."

"Ah, you are a biker chick!"

The smile creeps out with the memories this time, I can't help it. "I had a boy once. He liked bikes."

"Yeah? Where's he now?"

I shrug and swing my leg over and cop a seat on the pretty turquoise one I was eyeballing.

"Do you ride?"

"Dirt bikes," I say under my breath.

"This boy teach you that?"

I look up at him and change the subject. "So spill the details on the contract, Spence. I'm dying to know if this will work for me or not."

"OK," he says, taking a deep breath. "Come with me." I get up off the bike and follow him towards the back. There are a few lingering customers and one cashier helping people out, but the shop seems to be winding down for the day. He opens the door to an office that has his name on it. It says, *Spencer Shrike, President.* Which totally trips me out.

I walk in and Spence directs me to take a seat at a round table surrounded by cheap vinyl chairs that look like they belong in a VFW and not the Shrike Bikes president's office. I do, and then wait patiently as he gathers up some binders on the filing cabinet behind his desk. I look around the office as I wait. It's a typical biker office. Eagles and American flags, and of course, black velvet girls with tits hanging out, adorn the walls. I have to chuckle behind my fist because seriously…

I take my attention away from the artwork and study the furniture. The desk is a monstrosity of dark wood, mostly scratched and filled with paperwork. His office chair says a lot about him as well. It's leather, but not pretentious, and it looks well-worn, not new.

Spencer is a clash of contradictions. But this is a good thing. It says he's a down-to-Earth guy, not some asshole who gets off having the word *president* stenciled on his door.

He brings the binders over to the table and then takes a seat and looks over at me with a grin.

"What? You look nervous," I say.

He opens the book and there's an eight-by-ten glossy photograph of a naked girl. Except it's very hard to tell that she's naked on first glance because her entire body has been painted to look like she's wearing the sexy female version of an Elvis jumpsuit, complete with rhinestones and a nice sparkly belt.

I grin. "What's this?"

He turns the page and it's the same girl, only now she's wearing a roller derby outfit. He flips the page again and she's a cowgirl, complete with Wrangler jeans—it's an ass-shot—and a red checkered shirt.

The next page makes me gasp. Because it's a picture of Spencer, painting the girl.

"You!" I say, jumping up and grabbing the book from him.

"Me," he says proudly. "I paint on girls." We both laugh at that, hysterically almost. "I paint on girls," he says again. "And I want to paint a girl to match the custom bike I'm making for the Sturgis Rally this summer."

"Wow, you have blown me away, Spencer. Holy shit! Never in a million years did I think this was your secret. You're an artist!"

"Yeah, and I want to paint you, Rook. For the contract. I want to paint you to match all my bikes for the portfolio and advertising, but mostly, I want to paint you to match the custom bike I'm making special for Sturgis, because it's called the Shrike Raven. When I heard your name was Rook, well, that was it, girl. I just need it to be you."

"Wow," I say again. I nod at him. "I think I'm in, Spencer Shrike. This looks like the most fun I might ever have in my life."

"You'll be completely naked, Rook, just so you understand. When we do public performances, your nipples will be covered with those pasties, and you'll wear a thong, but that's only for the public appearances. In the photoshoots and in the private show at Sturgis, you'll be painted everywhere. And even with the pasties and thong, you have to be painted up nude, first. So it matches up perfect."

I flip through more pictures. Each one is perfection. You cannot tell these girls are naked. Not one bit. "I'm OK with that, Spencer. I'm in."

"Ronin is not going to approve."

"Who cares?" I reply, still flipping through the book.

"Well, I got the impression he liked you yesterday, so I figured you liked him too."

I can't hold it in anymore so I spill it. "I think he's seeing that Clare girl, Spencer. I saw them together today, in a bed. And we slept together last night. I thought we were, I don't know, together or something? But he obviously doesn't see it the same way. Maybe he *will* hate it, but I can't be bothered with that right now. I have to make my own decisions."

"Fair enough. I'm not gonna stop you, so you wanna see the bike you'll be painted up to match?"

"Yeah!"

We go back out to the showroom and it's empty now. He takes me to a book on the front desk and opens it. "This here is the showroom, but I build the bikes in a shop just north of Fort Collins, about a half hour from here. I'm almost finished with it, so we'll shoot you on the other bikes first, all painted up to match each one, and then we'll take the new bike to Sturgis and do a presentation to kick off the Biker Channel show we're gonna film for next year's spring TV season."

"Wow. I realize I've said that like three times already, but Spencer, you're amazing. This bike is the shit." Most of it is still in pieces, but the rendering is beautiful. It's got curves, and chrome, and the gas tank has been molded and painted to look like a raven's head.

"Which bike out here, Rook? Which is your favorite? You can pick one to be in the show too, then keep it for yourself."

I turn around and check them out carefully. "Are you serious?" I look at him, astonished.

"It's no big deal, these are showroom bikes, not special customs like the Raven. But I'll have it customized a little and we'll take it to Sturgis for you."

I walk between the aisles, my fingertips lovingly touching the tanks of several very nice specimens. But if I get to keep it, I should be practical so I can actually ride it. I don't want a chopper, that's for sure, they look difficult. I go back over to the turquoise one I was sitting on earlier and try it out again. "This one," I say, looking up at Spence's beaming smile. "I like this one."

"Can you really ride?" he asks as I lean forward on the tank and rest my cheek against the cool metal. I let my arms drop and a long sigh comes out.

"Yeah, I had a boy. He was wild about bikes."

"Hold on, be right back."

He leaves and comes back a few minutes later, pushing a cart filled with art supplies down the aisle. "Stay just like that, but lift your shirt up a little."

"What?" I laugh.

"I'll paint your back, just to make sure you know what you're in for. Just something simple."

I have to admit, this is exciting. "OK." I lift the back of my shirt up a little and lean back down on the tank. He sits behind me on the bike and grabs his supplies. First he washes my back with a wet cloth and then he dries it with a soft one.

"Now," he says, "tell me about this boy with the bike."

And I do. He paints while I talk. "Wade was his name. I was fifteen when I went to live with him. I was in foster care after my mom died, and this was literally like the tenth foster home I'd been in. I wasn't even a troublemaker or anything, it's just… I don't know, no one wanted me. Wade was two years older than me and he was a motocross racer. He taught me to ride a dirt bike and then he got a motorcycle when he turned eighteen and it was such a big deal. We had started messing around a little by then, and well, his mom figured I was bad news, a baby-maker waiting to happen maybe. She sent me away. But even though we never did anything beyond second base, he was my first love."

I wiggle a little at the soft touch of his brush on my back and he growls out a "Stay still, Blackbird," at me.

"And after that, Spencer, nothing in my life was ever good again until I found Antoine, Ronin and Elise last week." I stop for a moment to consider things, and then continue. "You too, I think. I mean I realize I barely know you, but shit, Spencer, you made my life today. Seriously, this whole offer is like a dream. And I've been pretty short on dreams these days, so it's a big deal to me."

He swishes his brush in a can of water and turns on a fan to air dry the paint on my back.

"Yeah, well," he says as he gets up and takes a seat on the bike next to me. I turn my head so I can see his face as we talk. "I have to admit, at first I just wanted to piss Ronin off and get you to agree, not that I didn't immediately think you were perfect, because Antoine described you over the phone. But Ronin and I used to be close and we're not anymore. So I was just being childish."

"So how do you two know each other?"

"We went to Catholic school together."

I almost choke on my own spit. "Oh shit, Ronin mentioned Catholic school last night, but I figured it was, I dunno, a weird suburban fantasy. How the hell did the two of you end up in Catholic school?"

"I always went to Saint Margaret's, since fucking pre-school. But Ronin showed up in eighth grade, just before we were about to graduate over to the Catholic high school. I lived in Park Hill and he lived over in the studio with Antoine. Ronin was a trip, ya know? He showed up out of nowhere speaking French like he grew up in Paris instead of Five Points, leaving school every few months to go travel the world for photoshoots. It was a strange life for a kid, but Ronin was never a kid. I found out about his parents a few years later when someone dug up the police report and plastered it all over school."

"Oh, that sucks. He told me about his father."

"Yeah, you'd think that would really piss a guy off, but not Ronin. He never even blinked. He said something in French, which roughly translated to *I am not my father's son*, and went about his business. That was tenth grade. We spent the next three years inseparable."

"What happened?"

"Ahhh," he says, getting up off the bike, "it's a long story. I better get you back before he goes apeshit. I have no idea what you saw today, but Ronin's not a cheater, Rook. He's just not. He's dated a lot of girls, I know that for sure, but he's never dated them at the same time. That's not him, so maybe let him explain."

He checks my back and pulls my shirt down after determining the paint is dry. I get up, feeling a lot better than when I left the studio, and I realize something.

I'm ready to go home.

Chapter Thirty-Seven

The studio is still bustling with activity when we arrive. It's hard to believe that it takes so long to unload bikes and roll them into the elevator and park them upstairs, but it must, because there are still two bikes in the truck.

We take the stairs and I'm exhausted because this day has been long and teetering on the edge of unpleasant since it started. If Spencer hadn't made this STURGIS offer, I'd probably be very depressed right now. We reach the fourth floor and the door is open, I can hear Antoine yelling in French about something. I'm really glad that guy prefers to get pissed in a foreign language, because it saves the rest of us from listening to his big-ass mouth.

"Rook! Where the fuck have you been?" Ronin yells, storming over to us.

"Spencer and I—"

Ronin pushes Spencer in the chest, sending him backwards, and then before I even understand what's happening they are throwing punches. "Wait!" I yell, grabbing at Ronin's arm. "What's the—"

Ronin reacts to my grab and pushes me away. I go flying backward and end up on my ass.

Again! That fucker!

Antoine pulls me up and asks me politely if I'm OK, and two of the technicians break up the fight.

"Where the fuck were you?" Ronin demands.

I ignore his question and turn to Antoine. "Spencer said he wants to offer me the STURGIS contract, so I'd like to sign that *right now.*"

I look over at Spencer, hoping I'm not overstepping my boundaries, and he smiles at me, still breathing heavy from the fight.

Antoine doesn't move, Ronin just stares at me, and Elise is the only one with enough sense to speak. "I'll get the papers."

"Rook, I think you need to wait on that, we can talk about this tomorrow."

"No, Ronin. I don't need to discuss anything with you. I got all the details from Spencer and I'm signing that contract tonight." *Because*, I don't add, *I'll be damned if I'm gonna get stuck here with an asshole who has pushed me down to the ground twice in the past fucking week while he was angry at another guy.*

Elise calls me into the office while the guys just stand around staring at me like idiots, so I walk off, then close the door behind me once I get inside.

"Sit," Elise says.

I do.

"Now, what happened? Last night you and Ronin were practically screwing each other in the rain, and today you disappear with Spencer and come back pissed off. What's going on?"

"It's got nothing to do with Spencer, if that's what

you're after. I'm just not sure I need a guy in my life, and to be honest, Elise, you're the one who warned me to stay away from Ronin. So I should be asking you the same question." I snatch the papers out of her hand, grab a pen off the desk and start skimming the stipulations. The contract looks like the last one so I assume it's standard and initial and sign in all the designated places.

I throw it down on the desk and take a deep breath and say in my most polite voice, "I'll move out as soon as I get paid for the TRAGIC contract. Can you give me an approximate time frame for that?"

She just sits on the corner of the desk frowning at me for a few seconds. "We have three more shoots to do, you can do them all tomorrow and we'll give you half. Then the other half once the final contract is delivered. But it will be a long day of non-stop work, Rook, and it's not the sweet kind either."

"I'll be fine. What time should I report?"

"Six AM."

I don't even nod this time, I'm just ready to be alone. So I spin on my heel and leave, walk past the men who stop arguing mid-sentence as soon as I emerge from the office, and head straight to my apartment. I set my phone to five AM so I can wash the crack whore off me before Elise and Josie can turn around and make me up as a meth fiend.

I'd forgotten all about the paint job Spencer did on my back yesterday, and I can't quite reach it to scrub it off in the tub. It doesn't help that I have to hold that damn shower head the whole time either, so I just leave it alone. I sigh, because I'm pretty sure this will piss everyone off if this is a naked day. I try to look at it in the mirror, and I can see that it's a dark bird that might be a rook or a raven, but it also has lettering down at the bottom, near the small of my back, and that is way too little to read backwards.

Well, what can I do?

Nothing, that's what.

When I walk out on the terrace it's still slightly dark, but all the lights inside the studio are on. I go inside and Elise, already busy with that tiny blonde girl, points to the dressing room and says, "See Ronin first."

Wonderful, he's the last person I want to see.

I walk into the dressing room and it's busy and filled with girls. All half-naked, all lining up at Dr. Ronin's scale to be weighed.

The bile comes up in my throat, that's how sick it makes me to think about this weighing-in stuff. And it's not because I'm worried about gaining weight. I might gain some, I might lose some, but I have a natural size to me and this is it. I'm not a fluctuator. It makes me sick because I can't stand the fact that he gets to invade me like this. It feels so…

"Get in line, Rook," Ronin says as I begin to wander off toward a bench that is not yet claimed.

I do what I'm told. I'm weak. There are only two girls ahead of me so it goes fast. I step on the scale without looking at Ronin.

He lets out a small laugh.

"What?" I ask.

"You gained two pounds." He laughs again.

"And you find that funny?" I ask, the irritation with him building.

"No, not funny. Just satisfying."

"Ugh! Where are my clothes?"

He points to a bag hanging from the rack with my

name on it and then whispers, "Don't get too comfortable in the clothes, though—it's TRAGIC, remember? Most of this day will be spent wearing nothing. And you better get used to it, *Blackbird*, because the entire STURGIS contract is nothing but full-body nudes."

I admit, this does make me uncomfortable, but then I remember the beautiful paint on all those nude girls in Spencer's book and relax a little about my decision. Besides, it's done. I signed the contract, it can't be undone without a huge production. And that's not something I'm interested in making.

I step off the scale and look around, not sure what to do next.

"Why are you doing this, Rook?"

"Doing what?" I ask, not looking at him.

"Taking another contract. It's clear that the shoot yesterday set you off, so why do more when you don't have to?"

I turn and meet his questioning gaze. "I do have to. I already told you, Ronin, I want to be independent and take care of myself. This," I say, waving my hand at the naked girls in the dressing room, "is a job that pays me money. And nothing more."

"So why disappear yesterday?"

"I did not disappear, I was with Spencer the entire time. Now, if you could just tell me what to do so I can finish this job and get the hell out of the garden apartment, I'd really appreciate it."

He watches me for a few more moments, then throws up his hands. "Go see Elise for make-up, then come back here and get changed."

Elise is shaking a thin white robe at me as I enter the salon, I grab it, go behind the partitioned wall to change, and come out wrapped up and ready.

"Shampoo," Elise says, pointing to the chair. I lie back and she turns the water on and begins, talking as she goes through the motions. "So, Spencer is nice, huh?"

I sigh. "I'm not interested in Spencer, Elise. Just his contract."

"Then tell me what happened. Ronin likes you, two days ago you liked him… how did you get to this place right now? It makes no sense."

She turns the water off and begins the shampoo. This time she is gentle, like the first time I showed up here. That was a week ago. One week, and this is what happens to my life. "I just don't think Ronin is the guy for me, that's all. I don't really feel like discussing it."

"And?" she prods, her fingers massaging the back of my head. "You have trust issues, right?"

I snort. "Elise, don't pretend you know me, because you don't."

"Well, I know Ronin found you huddled in the hallway like Clare was gonna kill you or something—" I bristle at the name and Elise senses this and stops talking for a second, then resumes her psychoanalysis. "And Ronin did manage to land you on your ass twice now out of jealousy, so I can see why you'd be pissed at him about that. And I know you were homeless when you ended up here, you admitted that to Ronin. And I know you've been hurt. So actually, Rook, while I might not know all the details, I think I know you better than you think." The water comes on again, saving me from responding, and I lie still as she rinses my hair. When she's done she squeezes the excess water out and applies the conditioner. "Today will not be pleasant, so just be prepared. I know you were unhappy yesterday with Billy, so at least it will be Ronin today, but it's going to be hard for you."

"Well, I'll get over it, Elise. Don't worry, I always do. By the time I have my life back on track and your door is hitting me in the ass, I'm sure exposing myself to cameras will seem second nature."

"But it doesn't have to be, Rook. That's what I'm saying. Ronin likes you a lot, just go with it. Why do that STURGIS contract? I can get you out of it, Spencer will be mad, but he won't make you—"

"Don't you *dare* try and talk him out of it! I will be so pissed!" Jesus! These people have some nerve! "I want that job, dammit! How many ways do I have to say it?"

She sighs heavily and rinses my hair out for the final time, plops a towel on it and sits me up. I get up and take a seat in her stylist chair so she can blow my hair out.

It's a long morning that bounces between uncomfortable silences and short curt responses and by the time Elise is finished with me, my musing about being made into a meth fiend is not far off when I look at myself in the mirror.

And that mirror is speaking to me.

It says, *Rook Walsh, you really* are *TRAGIC.*

Tragically stupid for agreeing to all of this stuff in the first place.

Chapter Thirty-Eight

Back in the dressing room I realize today's fun has only just begun. Ronin is nowhere to be seen, so I grab my bag and head over to the privacy stalls. Most of the girls are out in the studio by now, but I'm not interested in seeing anyone so the privacy stall it is. Inside the bag is the pink dress I wore for the very first shoot with Ronin. Well, maybe not the exact same dress, but at the very least, it started out looking just like it.

It's just that it looks nothing like that dress now.

Because the previously knee-length hem now falls just below my crotch and has a torn jagged edge. To my utmost delight the entire bust has also been modified, if you can call it that, because it's been cut out and replaced with black lace. Mix that all together with my tweaker make-up, some knee-high white stockings and black Mary Janes, and you've got Skanky Gidget Goes to Porn School.

My thong underwear barely qualifies as a postage stamp and since the bra is non-existent, it's just my nipples peeking through that, *cough*, amazing black lace.

Gross.

I turn around to look at my ass in the mirror, tug on the dress a little, and realize hoping for coverage is a lost cause.

"Well"—I spin around and find Ronin looking over the stall door—"I have to say, Gidge, I've seen you look better."

He opens the stall door for me and I scoot out and walk down the hall to the dressing room, then turn and give him a look-over. He's got different clothes on this time too—a pair of faded jeans, a white t-shirt, and black biker jacket. So he just gets to look like a hot greaser right out of *The Outsiders*. He's Matt Dillon as Dally and I'm still Skanky Gidget Goes to Porn School.

When I meet his gaze the sad expression on his face makes me feel shame.

But I'm a trooper, so I rally and paint on a smile. "Just tell me what to do so this day can be over and I can get paid."

"So that's all this is to you, a paycheck? That's all I was to you the other night? A paycheck?"

"I'm not talking about this, Ronin." I push past him and walk back out to the studio. Antoine, Elise, and a bunch of technicians are all waiting around for me. I catch Elise wince as she takes in my new look, but I ignore her and tip up my chin.

Ronin and Antoine are talking in French, not quite arguing, but not being amicable either.

Elise comes and takes me by the elbow, leading me over to the terrace. "Back under the cherry tree for you," she says as we walk outside. There are a lot fewer flowers on the branches now, most of the blossoms are on the ground, withered and wet from the recent rain. Elise lets go of me when we get to the swing and motions for me to take a seat. The technicians are already messing with the lights and those umbrella things, and then Ronin, Antoine, and the other photographers come out. I guess we wouldn't want to miss a single angle of my ass-crack, so yeah, why not get every single photographer we can, right?

Ugh. I want to die right now, and I'm not even naked yet.

Antoine doesn't speak a lick of English as we get ready, he talks only to Ronin and Ronin repeats everything he says in English for the rest of us. They start shooting right away and Ronin stays out of the picture for most of these. Then he stands behind me, tells me to move this way or that, and then kneels down in front of the swing, parts my thighs and lays his head along my leg. He's got a perfect view of all my goods and I just want to die all over again.

His hands reach under my ass and he turns his head up. "Look at me, Gidge. Antoine wants you to look at me."

I do as I'm told and I have to admit, it was a lot easier to do this when we were flirting with the possibility of a relationship.

"He wants you to be angry with me, but you already are, so I guess that's not a problem, is it?"

I just stare down at Ronin, my mind going a mile a minute.

"You mind telling me what I did?"

"I saw you," I say, as the cameras keep clicking.

"Saw me do what?"

"I saw you downstairs, in that apartment with Clare."

"Oh, fuck."

"Yeah, oh, fuck."

Antoine barks out an order to Ronin. "Get up,"

Ronin repeats after Antoine.

I do, and his hands are immediately around me, tugging me towards the tree. He leans back and pulls me into his chest. The cameras are clicking and Antoine continues to talk as Ronin's hands wrap around my ass and start to cup my breast. "It's not what you think, Rook," he whispers into my neck as his lips begin to kiss me.

I move away from his kiss and Antoine growls out something unfriendly.

"I have to, Rook, it's part of the shot. So just try and forget about all that stuff for now."

I keep my mouth shut and try to act like this is OK, but then he's unzipping my dress and pretty soon he's got one of my arms out, exposing my breast.

"You can say stop, you know," he reminds me.

"I know," I whisper. "But it's got to get done, right? So just go, just get it over with."

He continues with the other arm, slowly dragging the dress down until it falls to the ground and the tears are starting to build from the humiliation I feel.

"What the hell is on your back?"

Ronin's sharp words bring me back from the edge and I cover myself with my arms and turn away from Antoine. "The painting Spencer did yesterday."

Now Antoine is up next to me as Ronin spins me around so they can take a good long look at my body art. They both talk like I'm not there. And it's not even in French this time.

"Ah, fuck, Ronin! What the fuck is this?" Antoine growls.

"I didn't see it, she had clothes on at the scale!" Ronin retorts.

"Well, how the fuck are we going to shoot her with

this paint all over her back? Huh?"

"We'll just have to wash it off."

"It will make her skin red!"

"You guys do realize you're speaking English, right?" I ask. "I mean, I'm right fucking here!"

They switch to French and Elise brings me a robe so I don't have to stand there naked. "Come on, Rook, this shoot is over. We'll do it another day."

"But—"

"I'll still pay you half today, you can leave if you want, but we need to wash that paint off and this shoot is a disaster, so I'm calling *stop*."

That one word is all it takes. The crew begins packing up immediately, Antoine stops yelling, and Ronin grabs my hand and leads me back into the studio. He bypasses the dressing room and tugs me up the stairs, and before I can even string together a valid argument on why I should not be going into his apartment with him, I'm already there, sitting on the couch almost in tears.

Chapter Thirty-Nine

Ronin

I sit down on the chair opposite Rook in the living room and let out a long sigh as I drop my head into my hands, scrub my face and then look back up. "Tell me something," I ask, trying not to look at her in that make-up, "why do you think I weigh the girls? I mean, you've hinted that I'm some sort of control freak, so is this why you think I do it? So I can control you?"

Rook wraps her arms around herself. She's still naked under the robe and I take a minute to go get her a blanket from the hall closet. I offer it to her and she squeaks out a barely audible "Thank you," then pulls it up to her neck.

"You think I'm—what? Looking for girls who gain weight so I can fire them?"

"Aren't you?" she asks.

I laugh and shake my head. "Holy shit! No! I'm not looking to fire anyone for gaining weight, Rook. I told you, I don't care how much you weigh, I only care if you *lose* weight."

"You never said that, you said you were looking for a

weight *change*."

"Right, not weight *gain*." I stop again and lean back in the chair so I can look up at the ceiling as the guilt comes back. The guilt always comes back, and it always comes back to the same girl.

"There was a model who came through here a few years back. Mardee." I look over to see what Rook thinks about this, but she has her knees drawn up to her chest and her face is hidden in the blanket. "Mardee and I dated, I was only nineteen and she was just barely eighteen. Too young, really, like you, to be taking her clothes off for Antoine's camera. But like you, she did it anyway. And she was good at it.

"She got a lot of offers and pretty soon there were agencies and clients calling, she dumped me and started dating older guys, she got herself mixed up in a lot of bad shit and the worst of it was the drugs. In case you haven't noticed, this neighborhood is not the best. Sure, it's family friendly during the day and when there's a game in the stadium, but the reality of these streets is just half a block away. So she met some of the locals, all people I've known since elementary school, so you know, I was at the very least hesitant to tell her they were all a bunch of losers."

"What happened to her?" I have Rook's attention now and her eyes watch me carefully even as she tries to continue hiding her face in the blanket.

"She did a lot of heroin, that's what happened to her. She wasted away to nothing just as she started to make all her dreams come true. She ruined her life, she gave it all away for drugs. She'd show up here high as fuck and I pretended not to notice because I was in denial, or too busy to see how bad it was getting, or maybe, if I'm being honest here, I just didn't give a fuck about the girl beyond sleeping with her in one of the old rooms downstairs. And three months shy of her nineteenth birthday, she was dead."

"Oh, I'm sorry, Ronin."

"She died in one of our artistic rooms on the third floor. I fired her but I felt sorry for her after and let her stay in a room we rarely used. I found her down there, a tie-off still strangling her arm, the needle still sticking out of her vein."

I take a deep breath and then let it out and take responsibility for what I did. Maybe for the first time ever, I admit that this girl is gone because of me. "And not only did I know she was using, but I saw all the signs that she was *losing*. And the weight loss was the first clue. The weight loss, Rook, is the first clue in this business that something is wrong. And not just with drugs, either. With depression, and eating disorders, and all kinds of nasty things that plague people who rely on how they look to make their living.

"So that's why I check the girls every day. I'm looking to make sure that if they lose a pound or two, they gain it back pretty quick. Otherwise I start paying more attention to their habits and if I find out they're using, I fire them. That's the deal you signed on both of those contracts. I keep an eye on you for your own damn good."

I see her eyes flash, ready with the retort, but I'm way ahead of her.

"And if you think you can navigate this business alone, you're already dead, Rook. Because you *can't*. This business will use you up and throw you out like trash."

"So you think I'm stupid for signing Spencer's contract?"

"No, I get it. I really do. You got caught up in something bad and now you think money will save you from it ever happening again. And maybe it will, but money, from the way I see it, is the fucking cause of all the bullshit that happened to Mardee. If she had no money, she wouldn't have been able to buy drugs, or accept dates with rich losers, or sign contracts to do porn and whatever else she was doing at the end. Money won't save you, Gidge. Money is a tool and nothing else."

"Maybe," she admits. "But it's better to have bad options than no options. And people won't save you either, ya know."

I shake my head and let out a long breath. "God, that is the saddest shit I've ever heard."

She looks away now, her eyes glassy with the threat of tears. "No one came to save me. No one gave a fucking shit about me and the only reason I'm still alive right now is because I got myself out. I saved me, Ronin. Me."

I get up and join her on the couch. She turns her back to me so I push the blanket away and pull the robe down to look at the painting on her back. "Did Spence tell you what he wrote?"

She shakes her head and looks over her shoulder at me. "What'd he write?"

"He wrote, *I belong to Ronin and Spencer Shrike knows this.*"

"Oh, God!"

"It was meant for me, not you, Rook," I say, tracing the outline of the bird on her back. "He was sending me a message. We fought over Mardee. Spencer and I were best friends in high school and halfway through college, but I found out he was the one who introduced Mardee to the local scum dealers. Even though he grew up in Park Hill, he spent enough time down here with me to get to know them all. I pretty much poured all my guilt into hating him"—I stop to look Rook in the eyes—"so I could forget that it was really me who killed her. With my indifference."

She drops her head and sniffs.

"And I'd do anything to prevent that from becoming your future. But I can't stop you and honestly, I'm just a big fucking hypocrite because this is how I've made all my money too. This is how I bought into the partnership Elise and I have with Antoine. How I paid for this apartment, the cars, the truck, the bikes, the trips. I enjoy a lot of nice things in life because girls like you take off your clothes for guys like Antoine and me. So I've got no room to judge."

She sniffs again and the last thing I want is for her to feel defeated so I give her what she needs to hear right now. "But if you're going to take another contract, this body painting one with Spence is probably the best-case scenario because I know for a fact that Spencer Shrike is a good guy."

She looks over her shoulder, confused. "So you're not mad about that?"

"Fuck yes, I'm mad! But the truth is, Rook, you *don't* belong to me. You're free to do whatever you want. I can't stop you. I can give you my honest opinion, I can warn you when I see the dangers—but I can't make you do anything.

"And Rook, just so you know, I'm not looking for a girl to corner, or control, or use up and throw away. I've had that, I can get that anywhere. What I can't get anywhere is a partner who trusts me and loves me. So if you think I'm trying to trap you, you're wrong. I'm not interested in a girl who wants to get as far away from me as she possibly can."

She sits in our silence for whole minutes before turning her body so she can look me in the face. "I might like to belong to you, Ronin," she whispers. "Someday. But right now, I'm still running scared. A few months ago I looked at myself in the mirror and I had no idea who that girl was."

"You wanna hear a tragic story?" I ask Ronin, feeling ready to talk about it. "Because I really do have one."

He leans forward and kisses me on the top of my head, and then pulls me back into his chest. "Tell me, Rook."

"Well, one thing before I tell you, I just want you to know that I'm OK now." I wait to see if he has anything to add but I can tell he's just going to let me talk it out. "It's over, I'm gone, and I'm never going back. So, I'm not looking for anyone to go back and get him for me, or take pity on me, or any of that. But if I act a little distant or I make decisions that maybe don't fit with how you think, well, just know that I have my reasons. OK?"

He nods beneath me and I take a deep breath.

"Last year I was pregnant but I had a miscarriage. My ex caused it actually, and as terrible as this sounds, it was a blessing because not only did it prevent an innocent child from being born into a family of abuse, but I also got one of those implant birth control things while I was in the hospital." I pull the blanket away and rub my finger along my fleshy upper arm. "I knew what a baby with Jon meant and it wasn't an extension of our love or a chance to create something beautiful." I look up at Ronin. "It meant eternal captivity. He kept me locked in a prison—not the kind with bars and locks, but the kind that takes over your mind and holds you hostage. So I got the secret birth control implant because that was his plan. Get me pregnant and then use that baby against me for the rest of my life and hold me like a prisoner."

"Rook, I'm so sorry." He pushes some hair out of my eyes and kisses my head again.

I take a deep breath and continue. "I kept it secret for a while but one night while we were having sex, his hand was gripping my upper arm and he felt the little matchstick-sized implant. And he beat the living shit out of me. Pulled me up off the bed by my hair, slammed me down onto the ground, kicked me in the back so hard I thought I was paralyzed. Except I could feel the pain radiating up and down my spine, so I knew I wasn't paralyzed. I don't even know how many times he punched me in the face, I only know that both of my eyes were swollen shut long before he was done.

"When I didn't get up, he carried me to the shower, dropped me in the tub and turned the cold water on to wash away the blood. I could only lie there, motionless, or at least trying not to move because of the shooting pain going up my back. The water turned a dirty red color from all the blood spilling out of my nose.

"Usually, I never looked at myself afterward, but the next day I made myself. My face was unrecognizable—just swollen and—well, not me. And that's when I knew. If I stayed here with this man, he'd kill me. I'd be giving up my life if I stayed."

Ronin hugs me tighter and whispers into my neck, "And you left on a bus, all alone."

I nod. "After I was healed I left on a bus and ended up in Denver. It took exactly thirty-one days for my face to go back to the way it was. I wasn't working at that point, he made me quit my job long before then. So no one even knew. I had no family, I had no friends, I couldn't even ask a neighbor for help because we lived out on some land his family had. There was just this dumpy house in the middle of nowhere.

"But he gave me money every week so I could go shopping, before that beating anyway. And for three years I'd been planning for the day I'd have to leave because even though before that last incident I was too scared to really do anything about it, I knew that one day I'd have no choice. I knew that eventually he'd kill me. So I saved a few dollars from that allowance money he gave me when I could get away with it. Sometimes he checked my receipts and he kept a running inventory of all the food in the house, so it was very difficult to get enough to even buy that bus ticket, let alone a bit of money to get me through once I got away. He checked the mileage to make sure I never went anywhere in the car and he logged keystrokes on the computer to make sure I wasn't using it while he was gone. So I couldn't talk to guys or some stupid shit like that."

"He controlled everything."

"Yeah," I say. "He *owned* me." I turn around now so I can see Ronin as I talk. "And that's why I need this, Ronin. I need this, or I swear I wouldn't do it. You have to believe me. I don't want to do drugs, or stop eating, or make modeling my career. I have my own dreams and I'm not ready to give up on them yet. I just want the money so I can make my own decisions. And maybe this contract with Spencer is a mistake. Maybe I'll regret it, but I don't think so, because Spencer Shrike was gentle and he makes *art* on nude bodies. It didn't feel… dirty."

"Like TRAGIC."

"Yeah, this contract is definitely dirty. I mean of course I'll finish what I need to do to get paid, but I'm not interested in this modeling stuff, Ronin, I'm not interested in the clothes, or the attention, or anything like that. I just want the money so I can move on."

Ronin lies back on the couch and pulls me down with him so that my cheek rests on his chest. I'm still naked under the robe, but I don't care. He feels good.

"So you don't trust anyone."

"Right," I breathe. "I mean, I'm pretty well-adjusted I think. When I was at the shelter I talked to some counselors. It was very difficult at first, but every day away from him I healed a little more. And I know I have issues and maybe I'm making all the wrong decisions right now. That's possible, I get it. But even if what I'm doing is all wrong, I still need to do it. I need to be in control, I need to have these choices and I need to make my own mistakes. It's the only way to really make things right with me."

"But Gidge, you have to let people help you. You can't live in a vacuum."

"I know, I get that too. And maybe one day I'll trust someone else and let them take care of me again, but not today." I turn and look up at him. "That day is not today. I need a little independence, Ronin. I need to be able to think for myself. And honestly, I was about to give in to you after our date at the zoo and the night we spent together afterward. But then I saw you with that other girl and I realized that I'm just not ready yet. I'm way too vulnerable right now. I need a little more time, I need a little more control."

I relax back into his chest and we think things through in the silence.

"Well," he says a little while later, squeezing me a little tighter. "I'm sorry you had to see Clare and me like that, but I'm not dating her, Rook. I've never dated Clare. She's Antoine's niece and she's a mess. She came home high yesterday morning, that's her apartment, by the way. She lives here in the building. Antoine called me yesterday morning and I should've just told you what was up before I left you in bed, but I didn't. I'm sorry. Everything that happened yesterday was my fault."

He pulls back so he can see my face and I give him a little smile.

"Anyway, Clare has got a lot of problems and we were very close to getting her to check herself into rehab, so I stayed with her to make sure she didn't leave before the people came to pick her up. She's up in the mountains right now, hopefully she'll stay there and complete the program, but to be honest, she's been there before and nothing's helped."

He shrugs underneath me.

"She stresses us all out, you know? It's like, on the one hand we just want her to go away and kill herself somewhere else so we don't have to watch. But we can't let go. We let her come back, we take care of her, but it's not working. I don't think she's gonna make it, Rook, she's not strong like you. That day you showed up for your test shoot was the first time we let her model in months. And even though Antoine never lets her do anything but fashion and glamour shoots, we set her up for that sexy artistic shoot for one reason only. So I could check her body for indicators. And if I found anything that even hinted she was still using, we were gonna fire her for good.

"You take away the job, you take away the money, you take away the drugs. That's how it's supposed to work, right? How it should've worked with Mardee, too. The tough love routine. And maybe Clare just goes and finds her drugs somewhere else, but at least we're not contributing to it." He stops to exhale a long breath of air.

"But that day you showed up here I checked her over in the dressing room and she had fucking track marks between her toes."

Ronin just shakes his head and pauses for a few seconds. "That's a pretty bad sign. And we have no delusions, but Antoine figures we can't give up. So, I'm sorry she was the reason you were angry. If ever there was a girl who was tragic, it's Clare Chaput, not Rook Walsh." Ronin sits up and takes my face in his hands. "You're not tragic, Gidget. You're the sweetest thing I've ever seen. And I never want to see you in that ugly-ass TRAGIC costume again, but if you need this, and if you want to do the Shrike Bikes body art bullshit so you can stash a shitload of money away in some secret bank account and get some control over your life again, then just do me one favor."

"What?" I ask.

"Let me help you. Because I can make sure you get through to the other side intact."

I smile and whisper, "Thank you."

"But make me one promise, OK?"

"Now what, Larue?"

"That you'll listen and take my advice when I offer it. Because I can't help someone who doesn't want to be helped. I know better than most that it just doesn't work."

Even though I'm trying to joke, his face stays dead

serious. I swallow down my shame and give him what he needs. What we both need. "I promise, Ronin. I will listen and make good decisions based on your advice. Just don't give up on me yet because I really like you."

He pushes me off him and gets up, peels the blanket off of me and reaches down to slip off my clunky Mary Jane shoes. His hands glide up my calves and then tug down the white schoolgirl stockings. It takes all my willpower not to squeal at that, because it tickles so bad.

When he's done he takes my hand and pulls me to my feet, then leads me down the hallway. "Where are we going?"

"To wash the TRAGIC off you, Gidget. I can't stand to look at it for one more second."

He leads me into the bathroom and turns to the mission control panel that powers all the shower heads. They don't all come on at once this time, but a fine mist shoots out from the ceiling along with a puff of steam. He slides the robe down my shoulders and it drops to the floor in a soft whoosh and then undresses himself as I watch.

When we're both naked he opens the shower door and enter the mist of steamy water. He sits on the tiled bench against the wall and holds his hand out to me. I take it and climb into his lap as his hands dip down to cup my ass.

"I think you might've told a lie, Larue," I say playfully as I look down on him.

"Yeah? What'd I lie about, Gidge?" he asks innocently as he nuzzles my neck.

"This shower."

He tilts his head back and I smile.

"There is no way this shower is better than sex."

His laugh fills me up and suddenly I'm totally in the

moment. I tip my forehead down to his and squeeze my eyes shut to stop the happy tears.

The contracts can wait, Elise and Antoine can wait, life can wait. Because right now there is nothing else—there is no one else—in this world except us.

Rook and Ronin.

I'm not sure what's going to happen. Maybe we make it, maybe we don't, but if there's one thing I've learned, it's to appreciate the good when it happens. And having this man accept and want me the way I am right now is a good thing, and it's happening right this second.

So I'm gonna enjoy it.

To be continued…

Hey readers! If you enjoyed Rook and Ronin why not take a few moments to jot down a few words about the story and give it a rating on Amazon, because I'm an Indie and it's real hard to fight your way to the top of the pile where people can see you without a ton of reviews. So if you've got just a minute, I'd appreciate that.

Also - **Rook and Ronin, Book Two, MANIC, is scheduled to release on August 1, 2013**. You can add it to your Goodreads shelf right now and you can find me every single day over at New Adult Addiction Book Blog. That's where I post all my writerly updates and generally hang out with books, authors, and readers. :)

End of Book Shit

Take Two

Sometimes I make myself laugh. I'm getting ready to write up the acknowledgments and I figure, just go copy it from the last book, right? Switch it up a bit. But I had just lost my dog when I wrote that last one, plus it was a Junco book (which, if you've read them, is pretty self-explanatory), and I was in a really bad mood. So the title of the "Acknowledgments" section in the actual table of contents was End of Book Shit.

I forgot about that. Anyway, made me laugh. :)

This book I'm going to say thank you to the bloggers that have supported me on this whole writing thing. Namely, The Book Tart. Kat, I cannot even express in words how much I appreciate you. You are awesome, you have been a true friend to me, and I hope you know I really appreciate all that you've done.

Second, Bookworm Brandee. You totally made my week during the Range and Magpie release. Seriously, it was not a happy time for me, and you made everything better with your fangirl stuff. Thank you!

Also, I'm in a super fantastic private Facebook group for indie writers called INDIE INKED and they are the best group of ladies I've ever never met. :) Our collective goal is to rise to the top together, pull each other up. And it's working, we're getting there girls. :) I thank all of you for supporting me and bringing me up with you.

Special thanks to my family for being so independent and letting me sit down here in my office making up stories every day.

Finally, my editor RJ. I rely on you and could never have gotten any of these books published without you. Thank you.

WE ARE INDIE INKED

Just a group of Young Adult and New Adult authors writing in a range of genres from contemporary romance, science fiction, fantasy and paranormal. Check these ladies out, they are rising to the top quick!

Alivia Anders
Ella James
Cambria Hebert
Lizzy Ford
Anna Cruise
Angela Orlowski Peart
Julia Crane
J. A. Huss
Cameo Renae
Alexia Purdy
Tara West
Heidi McLaughlin
Melissa Andrea
L. P. Dover
Sarah M. Ross
Brina Courtney
Komal Kant
Melissa Pearl
Beth Balmanno
Tabatha Vargo
Amber Garza

If you like this book, you might like the other stuff I write (or maybe not, but you know, you should at the very least give it a look). Check out the first book in my Junco series.

ABOUT THE AUTHOR

JA Huss is a SF and new adult romance junkie, has a love-hate relationship with the bad boys, and likes to write new adult books about people with real problems. She lives with her family on a small acreage farm in Colorado and has two donkeys named Paris and Nicole. Before writing fiction, she authored almost two hundred science workbooks and always has at least three works in progress. Her first new adult romance is called TRAGIC.